The Shielding
Of
Mortimer Townes

MONTGOMERY THOMPSON

Copyright © 2015 Montgomery Thompson

All rights reserved.

ISBN: 1979092206
ISBN-13: 978-1979092203

DEDICATION

For Maksey, Anderson, Spencer, Paddington,
Josh and Michael; the kids of mom's kids.
Please... never stop being kids.

ACKNOWLEDGMENTS

Edited by Amanda Meuwissen
Assistant Editor Willow Wood

Chapter 1

Purple light made the steam glow, drifting sluggishly in the hot air as the entrepreneur's claws wrapped around his cool beverage. He brushed aside the little umbrella, his flicking tongue searching for the straw. Languishing in a hammock next to him was a five-foot long slug. Two shiny black orbs, perched on wobbly stalks and adorned with a thin strip of hair that passed as eyebrows, scowled in disagreement. It was a relationship almost as old as microbial life: lawyer and client consulting in the security of a private sauna.

"No," the slug drawled.

"What do you mean no?" His client, Sitasti, flicked his tongue in irritation; he didn't care for the word 'no'.

"There's no way, Sitasti, the law is clear. You can't develop any planet inhabited by intelligent life." The bulk of the lawyer's slugness shifted in the hammock leaving a disturbing grill-like pattern on his gelatinous skin.

"Drom, you know as well as I do that those primitives on Thun are nowhere near intelligent. Besides, none of the locals even knows they have company."

"Sitasti, I'm tired of this. Just because you stumble on an uncharted planet doesn't mean you get to enslave the natives. It's just not cost effective."

"You're right on that," he slurped from his umbrella drink, "the fines alone would put me out of business. Come on, you're my attorney.

Don't you know any loop holes?"

"No, Sitasti, the only way you're going to make a claim on that planet is if the inhabitants disappear and that's impossible, so just forget it."

Sitasti stood and began to pace. The seven-and-a-half-foot tall reptile scratched his scaly head and thought. Thun was his ticket to the big leagues. He had found it and named it. By rights, it was his, but he wasn't allowed to touch it.

"I don't like the concept of impossible, Drom. We're talking about an entire planet here! If I can work that claim, you and me will be rich beyond our wildest dreams. Think about it, your own private jungle, salt free! I might even be able to buy you a consulate seat." Sitasti leaned in close to the lawyer. "Imagine the look on Judge Blarck's face. You, taking your seat as an esteemed member of the Galactic Council."

"Blarck. That dahjkak. Putting his face in it would be worth a planet." The giant slug rippled with fury.

"That's what I'm talking about here. C'mon, Drom, an entire resource-rich planet is ours for the taking. The only thing that stands between us and our destiny is a few pesky natives."

Drom deflated. "But it's an impossible obstacle. If you touch them, and I mean if they even see you, the Council will lock you away. Section Ten lays it out as clear as drool." Drom cleared his throat. "And I paraphrase: 'There is only one instance where a non-native is even allowed on an undeveloped planet and that would be to protect the natives from deliberate harm by a non-native intelligence'. Even then, you're not allowed to be detected by the natives. Oh, and here's the important part, Sitasti—upon penalty of life imprisonment!"

But Sitasti wasn't listening. He was staring at a faraway place, his synapses firing like bubbles in a boiling pot of oatmeal. He whirled around and looked at Drom wild-eyed and salivating; he had an idea. A toothy grin broadened on his face as he raised himself up and waggled a stubby finger.

"There's one thing I've learned, Drom, my old friend: Impossible is the only thing that's impossible. If I can't enslave the primitives, I'll get rid of them or…" From the bubbling oatmeal of his brain another idea surfaced. "…better yet, I'll make it so they get rid of themselves. Remember that guy we hired to take care of those protesters?"

"You mean the guy I hired for you. Yeah his name was Ilgut." Drom chuckled. "He really made a mess of those punks. I can't believe he didn't get caught."

"Ilgut, right, find him and tell him we've got another job for him. And tell him to pack for a short jump across the sector."

***

Across the galactic sector on a planet with two moons called Thun, in the country of Fremia, in the province of Rucksuit, in the county of Vangs, in a little town called Legly that looked remarkably similar to a small 1960's English village but wasn't, a little girl named Maksey tried to shove her head into the street drain.

"Did you see that?" She pushed and kicked as water cascaded around her head. On the street, her older sister Shaley pulled on her feet to keep her from falling in.

"Are you crazy? You can't go in there! Maksey, stop it, I swear I'll tell Mom!"

"It was a huge snake man! He had a packsack on with a big gun. He went that way through the sewer!"

Their older brother Spence had been sent to round them up for dinner. The rain began to fall heavier, pelting them with large drops as dusk receded into evening.

"You dapes. It's getting dark and we're getting soaked. Get out of there and come home, now!

Maksey gave one last push to try and fit into the drain but it was no use. Whatever she had seen was long gone. She sat up, her dark hair was dripping wet and covered in leaves and dirt.

"You saw him didn't you?" she asked her siblings.

Spence just rolled his eyes.

"There was nothing to see, Maksey, just you trying to drown yourself. Mom's gonna ground you for a year!" Shaley picked her bike up from the pavement.

"He was real! I saw him look at me. He was black and green and kinda yellow all over, and had a pack-sack on his back—"

"Yeah yeah, with a big gun, we know, Maksey, you told us already." Spence stood her up and flopped her hood over her head. "Now let's go!"

Maksey stomped back home, following her brother. The snake-man was real, she'd seen it. Mom would be mad that she was crawling in the mud and water, but when she heard about the incredible thing Maksey had seen, she couldn't stay mad for long.

Maksey marched on behind Spence and Shaley, her face set in scowling determination.

***

Mim stood in the open door of her small council house and stared out into the rain. Out on the street, her three children walked towards the house. "What are you doing? Hurry up, you're getting soaked!" she yelled.

The kids picked up speed and burst through the door in a tumble of wet raincoats and shoes.

"Maksey, what are you doing out there in the pouring rain?" Mim scolded. "You'll catch cold and you know we can't afford a doctor right now."

Spence pulled off his overcoat. "She had a raincoat on, Mom." The fifteen-year-old dropped his soaking coat on the floor and stomped off to the kitchen.

"Mom! Maksey was trying to climb into the sewer—"

"Shaley!" Maksey turned red at her sister's betrayal. She should have known; Shaley was such a tattler.

"But I told her not to, and Spence was telling her that she should and—"

Mim put her finger to Shaley's lips. "That's enough Shaley. I've told you before, no one likes a tattletale."

"But, Mom!"

"Enough, Shaley. You should have been helping Spence get Maksey back inside. You're supposed to be looking out for her. Now," she pointed, "to the kitchen, go."

Shaley rolled her eyes and plodded off to the kitchen while Mim picked Spence's coat up of the floor.

"Maksey, what were you thinking trying to climb into the sewer?" Mim asked.

Maksey stuck her tongue out at the back of her twelve-year-old sister as she tugged her coat off. "I saw a big slimy snake-man, but when he saw me he swam away."

"A big snake, huh? You didn't ask him his name?"

"Mom! I'm serious!" Maksey's face screwed up in frustration. "He had a big pack-sack on his back and a gun sticking out of it and—"

"All right, all right, maybe you can draw a picture of him for me after dinner. Now dry off and get to the table." Mim sighed. Maksey was ten and, much to Mim's distress, seemed to have no fear of anything.

She hung up the coats and followed her children into the kitchen as evening settled over Legly.

***

Relieved that the youngling was gone, Ilgut pushed his large, snake-like body through the pipe with a low grunt as he made his way through the sludge to the edge of town. The lawyer, Drom, had promised an easy job, but nothing was ever easy when he worked with that dahjkak. He had been grunting his way through sewers since he arrived on this backwards planet.

After narrowly dodging the interest of that overly inquisitive young native, he had pushed through the pipes for another half an hour until finally he peered out of the drain through a small black scope and looked across a large field surrounded by woods on three sides. A small brick farmhouse stood just off the road and he could see two natives inside, both elderly.

"Perfect."

Grey light dimmed in the evening sky; it would be fully dark soon. Ilgut slid back down into the muck and waited.

***

Inside the sturdy farmhouse, an old farmer and his wife settled in for an evening in front of the tele, as they did most evenings. Mortimer's enduring frame creaked as he bent to fidget with the antennae on the television. Nearly deaf and mostly blind, he struggled to get a clear signal, which seemed to stubbornly evade his efforts, but the thin old man persevered. Finally, he straightened and returned to his faded armchair, satisfied with the picture.

His wife Aga, equally as impaired as Mortimer, carefully brought in their evening meal as she always did. Mortimer lovingly took the meal from her, and when she had settled into her seat, said a prayer of thanks.

On the TV, the news anchor intoned soberly, "The top story tonight: the Fremian Leadership Council votes fifty to two in favor of trade sanctions against Olred in response to allegations of spying. The allegations rose from what Olred claims was unauthorized aerial activity in restricted Olred airspace. Fremian military officials maintain that although they confirm that they also detected the activity in Olred airspace, it was in the outer atmosphere and too high for any Fremian planes to operate. We go now to our aeronautical correspondent for more…"

Mortimer reached over and touched his wife's hand. Outside the humble farmhouse, at the edge of the field, the birds stirred in their sleep.

***

Namarin Road ran past the Townes farm and ventured further out into Vangs County. The only car on it that evening belonged to Sgt. Bemis, the head of Legly's two-man police force. He told his wife he had taken on the added responsibility of the evening patrol because it was what a good leader did. In reality, it was an excuse to wait for his wife to go to bed. If he showed up at home before then, the woman would drown him in an unfordable river of babble.

It would start as a trickle with the women at the salon, then turn into a stream of talk about who died recently or who wore what at bingo night. Soon the stream would merge into a river as she went through every inhabitant of Legly, their questionable lifestyles and likely misdeeds. The river would swell into a flood as she assigned him police duties to spy on the rumored offenders, she might even try to get him to arrest people in their homes. The woman wasn't right in the head.

No, he shuddered; it was best to stay on patrol. He shifted his police cap on his head and made his way back into town, happy to have an excuse to not be home. As the old police cruiser ambled towards the town center, he didn't notice the large uncoiling shape rising in the darkness behind him.

***

Ilgut let the rain wash the sewage off him as he stared after the police car. "Primitives," he snorted, and then slithered off the road and across the lawn of the small farmhouse.

His eyes pierced the dark as he scanned for native animals, but there were only grazers out in the field. Silently, he coiled next the window of the house. Inside he could see Mortimer and his wife watching television.

"Black and white," he scoffed, "what a loser. This guy is definitely my target."

His biological combat implant scanned and then locked onto the old man. Once a target was locked, it could go anywhere in the galactic sector and the assassin would be able to locate it.

Ilgut crept into the woods at the edge of the farm to wait until daybreak. He needed witnesses when the old guy snuffed it.

Chapter 2

Constable Pal Tember shook his head as he examined the evidence. Bemis was slumped at his desk, snoring away. The overweight Police Sergeant was still in uniform, which was covered in crumbs, but there was no smell of alcohol on him. All of the donuts, of which there had been twenty-two at the end of the day yesterday, were gone. The keys to the cruiser were on the desk and the cruiser itself had obviously, due to the dry patch under it, been parked all night.

"Donut coma."

Sgt Bemis snorted and started awake. "Wha?"

"A donut coma," Tember said loudly. "It's a clear and shut case. You didn't go home last night. Instead you came in here after you got bored on patrol, ate the rest of the donuts, and fell asleep."

"Alright, rookie, that's enough out of you." Bemis sat upright and brushed off the crumbs.

Tember cracked a smile. "Just saying, Sarge. It's no big deal, just doing a bit of sleuthing that's all."

"Yeah well, you don't know anything. Now get to work before I find something for you to do."

"All right, no need to get all grumpy, I'm on the job," he said, retreating to his desk across the room.

"Good, that means I can go and get a fresh uniform. I'll be back soon."

Yeah right, Tember thought, *as soon as you get a nap and a shower.*

***

Spence looked over his shoulder. Shaley was trying to catch up with him, and Maksey was close behind. The sun was making a big to-do about morning, though it was still a bit chilly. Mim had sent Spence to the store for milk with express orders to take the girls along, but Spence knew that if he left them behind, he could spend the change on a candy bar.

"I'll tell Mom you're trying to ditch us!" Shaley trotted after him.

"Go ahead, you little pest, she'll just tell you not to be a tattletale." He reached back and tweaked her nose. The pain made her stop and cry out. Spence increased his speed to a jog.

Shaley watched her brother disappear down the street; now she would never catch up with him. Just then, Maksey came trotting up.

"What did he do?"

"Nothing, he's just being a shik." Shaley rubbed her sore nose. "Come on, we'll find something better to do." Shaley turned and started back to the house.

Half an hour later they sat on the front stoop tossing the odd pebble at puddles leftover from last night's rain, feeling dejected and bored. Suddenly Maksey's face brightened.

"Shaley, look!"

A gang of five boys that usually congregated on the next block rode by on their bikes, looking very much like they were up to no good.

"Let's follow them!" Maksey was already getting her bike from storage under the stairs.

"I can't, Maksey, my bike is broke," Shaley said, looking for an excuse not to go.

"We can ride doubles on mine."

"But—" Shaley began to protest but it was too late, Maksey was already starting to pedal off. Shaley caught her, climbed on, and took over pedaling. She was the older one after all.

The sun grew stronger as they rode. Maksey held onto the back of the long seat while Shaley pedaled furiously to catch up with the pack of boys.

"Don't get too close, we don't want them to know we're following them," Maksey said in a serious tone.

"Right." Shaley slowed her pace a bit.

They followed the boys past a small lake, then another row of council houses. The sun felt good as the fresh air whipped through their hair. Shaley went faster. They leaned into a bend that took them past the auto garage and straightened into a long, steep hill that intersected Namarin Road. Shaley pedaled hard as the bike began to climb the hill. Hauling back on the handlebars she pushed until her legs came to a standstill and they had to get off the bike and walk to the top. By the time they got there, the pack of boys had disappeared.

"Oh great," Shaley said, catching her breath.

"Which way did they go?" Maksey looked down the empty road both ways but there was no sign of the boys. She stepped into the road to try to get a better look. As she strained her eyes, she saw that the road went through a tunnel of old trees. The sun glinted off the wet road and she caught the briefest flash of a group of thin lines drying on the pavement.

"There! I see it! They went this way!"

Both girls scrambled onto the bike and Shaley worked the pedals hard. Soon they were riding through the tunnel of trees, the cool air giving them goose pimples on their arms. As they broke out into the sunlight, Shaley spotted their quarry in the distance and came to a stop.

"What are they doing?"

"I think they're coming back this way," Maksey said, trying to see over Shaley's shoulder. The girls watched them for a minute, and sure enough, the gang of boys was getting closer, and fast. "What are they yelling?" Maksey gave Shaley a confused look.

"I don't know. They're boys, they're all kinda weird."

The bicycle boys came at the girls with fear in their faces in a frenzy of pedaling and yelling, flying past like a demon was on their tail. Shaley just looked at her younger sister and shrugged.

Maksey shook her head. "Weird."

***

Ilgut the snake assassin never slept. As the night passed overhead silently, he remained motionless, watching from the limb of an old tree on the forested borders of the Townes' farm.

Eventually the sun rose and Mortimer woke. Ilgut's tracking sensor stayed locked on to his every move. The red cursor pinpointed the old man's location inside the house, even through the walls, but Ilgut would have to wait for a shot.

His orders were clear, choose an upstanding citizen, a complete innocent, then take him out. Make it a spectacle with lots of witnesses. Ilgut had no idea why they wanted it like that, but with the kind of money he was getting paid, he wasn't about to argue. All he had to do was make the hit and slip away quietly. Zero contact, that was the deal. It would be simple with these primitives, he thought. There was no way they could even comprehend what was about to happen.

An hour went by and Mortimer came outside to mow the lawn. He moved slow and sure, taking his time in everything he did. At first, it mesmerized Ilgut. The methodical rhythm of Mortimer's puttering brought a kind of ritual to the most mundane of tasks. Eventually though, it began to irritate the assassin. There was too much perfection, simplicity and patience. He wanted to pull the trigger right then and there, but he knew he had to wait for witnesses.

He quietly cursed a string of obscenities as he watched Mortimer mowing, back and forth, making a perfect crisscross pattern in the perfect grass.

***

For Chalo the bike was freedom, a way to get as far as possible from his step-dad. He and his friends were the heroes of Legly; Legly just didn't know it yet. Every one of his little gang wanted to be a superhero. Besides the bikes, comic books were their thing. At thirteen, Chalo was the oldest, and therefore the leader. Then came Inder, a tall blond kid, fearless and, Chalo thought, kinda goofy. Regin was the big one, the muscle of the gang, even though it was mostly fat. Running a close tie for last place was Ob and Gern, the twins and the youngest of the bunch though not by much.

As the summer wore on they'd become bored with their normal haunts and started riding further afield. Today, Chalo decided they would take Namarin Road all the way to the next town. It would take over an hour of hard riding to get there, but it was time to do something epic.

After a planning meeting in Chalo's garage, complete with a model map made out of random objects to show their route, they saddled up and headed out. Everyone stayed in their designated riding order: Chalo in the front, then Regin followed by Ob and Gern with Inder, the second in command, taking up rear guard to make sure Ob and Gern didn't lag behind.

The hill proved the most difficult part of the ride, but they made it up to Namarin Road and took the left turn that headed to the town of Pelgar. Pelgar was almost twice the size of Legly and their rival in almost everything, but they also had a bigger selection of everything, including comics.

The boys put their backs into it and kept a good pace. Passing under the tree tunnel, they approached the Townes' farm on the right. It was the last residence before the thirty-minute ride to Pelgar. Chalo pulled over at the planned resting spot right at Mortimer's front gate. The old farmer was mowing the lawn just twenty feet away and waved at them while the boys passed around a canteen of water. Chalo coolly raised a hand to him.

"Hey there, old guy, how's it going?"

Mortimer just smiled and waved.

"You can't hear a thing I'm saying can you?" Chalo said through a tight-lipped smile. "Yep, just nod and smile." But his expression changed suddenly when a bright red light flashed out of the trees and exploded behind the old farmer.

Regin fell off his bike and Ob and Gern screamed. Before Chalo could react, three more bolts of light smashed into Mortimer in a series of sharp cracks. Each impact revealed a transparent sphere surrounding the old man that protected him from the blasts. Mortimer paused mid-wave and puzzled at the boys' reaction to him. Chalo dropped the canteen and pedaled so hard he peeled out in the dirt. It wasn't until they passed the two girls at the edge of the trees that he realized he had been yelling.

***

Ilgut had been waiting for his chance. He needed witnesses and finally it looked like he was going to get his wish, a group of younglings had just arrived at the old man's gate. The weapon silently raised into place on his back as his cursor controlled the aiming. The thin rail of the weapon began to glow dark red as it followed the bobbing of Mortimer's head. Then the target stopped and waved to the younglings. When they saw him and waved back, it was the confirmation Ilgut needed.

With a thought, the weapon fired, sending an explosive bolt into his target with enough force to melt a battle tank. But when the smoke cleared, the old man still stood. Ilgut was stunned. Was that a shield? He fired three more times. This time he looked hard for the spherical shape that repelled his shots. Sure enough, a shield.

He cursed and slithered out of the tree. It was a setup. He should have known! Drom, that dahjkak! What did he do, hire someone else to make sure the job was done? His mind searched for possibilities as he dove through the underbrush, seeking cover. What were the chances that another assassin would pick the same target? Slim indeed. This was a setup.

After several minutes, Ilgut found a small pond just big enough to get into. He shuffled back and forth to settle into the mud while he scanned the trees for the source of the shield. Just as he had settled in, he went completely weightless. Arms, legs, and claws scrambled to hold on to something, anything as he rose rapidly out of the pond. Mud flew off of him as he lashed violently to get free, but it was no use. He knew he was caught in a tractor beam.

Ilgut was hauled up like a worm on a hook, accelerating at a blistering speed through the upper atmosphere and into the belly of a Unified Galactic Police cruiser.

***

The boys on their bikes faded in the distance. For Maksey, the allure of the mystery was too much to resist. "Let's go see what scared them!"

Shaley reluctantly agreed.

They pulled up at the farm entrance and parked behind the hedge. The old man had resumed mowing, completely unaware of the assassination attempt.

"What were they freaking out about?" Shaley looked at Maksey who was wide eyed, watching something in the sky.

"That's him! That's the snake-man I saw in the sewer! He's flying!"

Shaley turned and saw Ilgut, zipping upwards into the sky and finally, getting so high he vanished altogether. Her head snapped back to Maksey, eyes like saucers.

Maksey just looked at her and smiled.

Shaley's head snapped back, her eyes, large as moons, fixed on the sky. She felt the bike shake as Maksey jumped off and started running towards the trees.

"C'mon Shaley!"

"Maksey! Come back here!" Shaley ran after her.

***

Far across the field a small chuckle drifted out from the trees as Sitasti watched Ilgut disappear into the sky.

"Perfect, absolutely perfect." It had been easy to link to Ilgut's antiquated targeting system. Once the assassin had targeted Mortimer, Sitasti knew where to set the shield. Pleased with his plan, the entrepreneur retreated into the woods a short distance then checked his cover.

The shield had worked so far, but he would need to keep it charged for the job ahead. The thing looked like it could have been a prop from *The Jetsons*; a simple box with a thick cable attached to a gun with a small dish at the end. Sitasti opened a panel on the box and manipulated a set of controls. On the backside of Thun's smaller moon his ship responded to the commands.

Thun had two moons, but only one was visible in the day, the other was very small and growing smaller as the years went by, as it faded from the planet's gravitational grip. In a few hundred years it would be gone altogether. For now it served as the perfect place to hide his ship from the ever-snooping Unified Galactic Police (or the UGPo for short).

Going through a series of checks he made sure that the police cruiser was out of the area then maneuvered his ship into geo-stationary orbit above his location. It only took minutes for an invisible beam to charge the shield generator.

Sitasti kept an eye on Mortimer; he had to insure the old man remained indestructible at all costs.

Chapter 3

As evening settled over Legly, Mim stood at her front door scanning the streets. Spence had returned without the girls and was in serious trouble for ditching them. They weren't home yet. Worse, no one had seen them and her stomach churned with worry. She had just been out driving around the whole town looking for them and was about to turn and call the police when a group of boys rode by the house on their bikes.

Mim was used to the strange antics of the little gang of boys from the neighborhood, but tonight they were weirder than usual. They had strapped what looked like tin foil covered medieval shields to their handlebars and the bikes were covered completely in the stuff. They glanced nervously at Mim as they whisked past the house.

"Hey! Boys, wait a minute! Boys?"

They sped up and disappeared down the street. Mim, at the height of worry and frustration, went in the house and dialed the police station. Sgt Bemis answered, took some basic information, and promised to send his constable out to get a full description of the girls as soon as possible.

Ten minutes after hanging up the phone, she heard the police car pull up.

***

Pal Tember fidgeted with his paper pad as he went to the door. He hated 'missing person' calls. It meant having to tell someone that they would have to wait, then they would cry. It was all so uncomfortable and disappointing. They just didn't have the staff to search the town. He reached out to ring the bell, but the door opened before he could. Tember stood slack jawed, staring at Mim. She was lovely.

"Constable, my girls are missing. Maksey is twelve and Shaley is fourteen." She thrust a framed photograph into his hands. "I've been everywhere but no one has seen them. You have to find them for me. It's getting dark and they're just little girls—"

"Alright, ma'am, we'll do everything we can. I just need some information—"

"Information? There's the picture, what else do you need?" Mim reached behind the door and lifted her coat off the hook. "I'll go with you. They know my voice. I can call for them from the air. You do have a public address system on the helicopter, don't you?"

At six-foot four Tember wasn't used to being bulldozed by anyone, let alone a delicate five-foot five lady, but he just didn't have the heart to tell her that there were only two policemen in the whole town and they certainly did not have a helicopter.

"Easy there, ma'am, just calm down, I'm sure we'll find them."

"That's easy for you to say! I've looked in every corner of Legly, down every street and alley way, and I still couldn't—"

"Okay, I understand, but we have to follow protocol to give us the best chance of finding them." Tember took the coat and held Mim's trembling hands. He really felt for her; she was frantic. He looked her in the eyes to show his sincerity. "Just come in and sit down, it will only take a few minutes to get the search started. Please, ma'am, help me help you."

Something in the constable's eyes eased her frayed nerves. She took a deep breath and conceded. "Yes, maybe that's best. Thank you. I'm Mim."

"Tember, Constable…just call me Pal." She was even more beautiful when she wasn't panicked.

She sat him on the couch and told him what she knew, but had to admit that they could have gone anywhere. Tember was at a loss. He wanted to help her more than anything.

"Is there anything else you can tell me?" He shrugged. "Maybe anything unusual around the neighborhood or...?"

"Yes, now that I think of it there is one thing." Mim told him about the boys and their odd behavior. "When I hear myself tell it, it sounds like it's just boys being boys, but this was different. They were scared and, odd as it sounds, looked like they were on patrol or something."

"Right. We'll start there. I'll talk to them and see if they know anything. I'm sure they won't be hard to find. And your son, Spence is it? You're sure he's not holding something back to keep from getting into more trouble?"

"No, he's definitely been forthcoming. He may be a typical teenage older brother, but he loves his sisters and would never do anything to jeopardize their safety." She thought of her little girls all alone in the dark night somewhere and burst into tears.

Tember had known it was coming, but he didn't mind as she reached out and took his hand.

"Please Constable...find them. They're just children."

"Don't you worry, I'm on the job. I'm going to find those boys right now."

***

Tember left the house and circled the neighborhood in his cruiser. He didn't have to go far before he saw the tin foil covered bikes outside of a small, ramshackle house. Light spilled from the seams of the garage door. As he approached, he could hear the kids' voices inside the garage.

"Excuse me, boys, do you mind coming out here for a minute?"

He was answered by a sudden rustling on the other side of the door as the light in the garage went out. He shook his head and sighed.

"It's all right, you're not in any trouble. I was just hoping that maybe you could help me solve a special case I've been working on."

The garage stayed quiet. He could hear them breathing.

"It's hero kind of work. I could sure use the help of a few heroes to help make one of our citizens very happy."

A small shuffling noise, then the garage door lifted open as the boys came out one by one.

"Quite a clubhouse you've got there. Much better than the one I had when I was your age. Now, tell me, have you seen two little girls today?"

"They were in the tunnel of trees by the farm up on Namarin Road."

"When was that, do you remember?"

"It was around two, but we just passed them, we don't let girls ride with us."

"I see, anything else?"

The boys exchanged worried glances. "Nope."

"You're sure?"

"Uh huh."

"Alright then. Thanks for your help. If you think of anything else you can call the station."

The boys were clearly relieved that the meeting was at an end. Tember drove straight to Mim's and told her what he had learned.

"That's the Townes' farm. Mister Townes might have seen them." The frantic look had returned to Mim's eyes and she grabbed her coat and pushed Tember out the door.

"Heck, maybe they're over there having pie or something," Tember offered as they climbed into the cruiser and sped out toward the farm.

***

Mim had never been in a police car before. It smelled official and, considering the circumstances, a bit frightening. She attempted some small talk to pass the time and distract her nerves.

"So, how long have you been a policeman?"

"About five years." He cleared his throat. "Mim, can I ask you a personal question?"

She was hoping he would. "Sure, why not."

"How is it an attractive woman like yourself, with three fine children, ends up alone?"

"Oh. Well, my husband died."

"I'm sorry, I—"

"No, it's okay. I haven't spoken to anyone about it for so long. Rale was a logger. One day he went to work and they say…he just wasn't paying attention and…well, logging is a very dangerous job. That was five years ago."

"Well, I'm going to do everything in my power, both professionally and personally, to find your girls."

Mim wondered what he meant by 'personally'. He was a nice man; nice smile, nice demeanor, and…she blushed a bit, nice to look at, but right now all she wanted was her girls safely back at home.

***

Mortimer's driveway came into view and Tember parked the cruiser. It took a few minutes for the old man to answer the door and then a bit of shouting as they explained the situation to him. Mortimer told them that he had indeed seen the girls. He gave them a large flashlight and told them that they were welcome to search anywhere they wanted. He would help by checking any of the outbuildings on the property.

Mim and Tember went across the fields and into the woods, calling the kids' names. It took over ten minutes, but finally the girls came bounding through the trees toward them.

"Mom! Mom! Here! We're here!"

After a joyous reunion of hugs and tears, Mim asked them, "What in the world are you doing all the way out here?"

"Maksey ran into the woods after we saw the boys go by. They were really scared!"

Tember looked at Mim, perplexed.

"That's Maksey," Mim told him. "She has no concept of fear and runs straight into danger. Her curiosity gets the better of her."

"But, Mom, I saw him, the snake-man! He went up to the sky like WOOOSH! Didn't he, Shaley? Shaley saw him too!"

"What is she talking about, Shaley?"

"Nothing, I don't know. She just ran into the woods and I tried to keep her out of trouble, but she got us lost. She just kept running around everywhere like a nut case."

"That's not true! You saw him! I know you did! There was slime in the tree and everything! Mom…" Maksey burst into tears but Shaley refused to admit that she had seen anything out of the ordinary.

Mim was siding with Shaley, but Tember was sure the older girl wasn't telling the whole story. He decided to stay out of it. All that mattered was that the girls were safe.

Chapter 4

The next day, Inder was reclined on the old couch in the clubhouse, reading a comic. "That was so close. I can't believe your dad didn't wake up."

Chalo surveyed the map from their unaccomplished ride. He had just finished adding on Mortimer's field and as much of the surrounding forest as he knew. "The cops don't know anything about it. They were just looking for those stupid girls. We've got bigger fish to fry, boys. It's time to ramp up the operation."

"Whaddaya mean, Chalo?"

"I mean we're going back to the farm."

Regin struggled to figure out their leader's logic for a moment, when it came to him. "Yeah," Regin agreed, "if the old man has powers, that means he's a superhero, probably retired."

Ob and Gern sat up at this revelation.

"Really?" they said in unison.

"Whoa…maybe he could train us and tell us how we get our own powers!"

"Regin, don't be a shik brain. That old fert didn't even know what was going on. Did you see him?" Chalo parodied Mortimer, making a stupid face and waving. "Derr, I'm just a dumb farmer. What? Is somebody shooting at me? I don't see anything!" The boys howled with laughter at Chalo's antics. To them, Mortimer was just a feeble old man with no sense of how the real world worked. "We're going back, but this time we're going to be prepared."

"What do you mean?" Regin asked.

"Know your enemy." The other kids just looked at each other like Chalo had started to lose it. "Ob, Gern, doesn't your dad have one of those new movie cameras?"

"Uh huh."

"We're going to need it."

"No way!" said Gern. "He'll kill us! He just got that thing. If he finds out he'll—"

"I don't care! This is for the team. The fate of the world depends on us. You saw what happened; that wasn't a normal gun. That was like a force ray, like this." He snatched Inder's comic from him. The cover was a picture of a superhero holding a shield against an alien attacking with beam weapons. The boys swallowed and looked out at their bikes with the flimsy cardboard and tin foil shields.

"Don't worry, we're not going there to fight that thing," Chalo said. "I'm more interested in the shield on that farmer. We need evidence if we're gonna get anybody to believe us. So, Ob, Gern, you have to get that camera." Ob and Gern nodded, wide-eyed, and took off on their bikes. "And don't forget the film, you dapes!" Chalo shouted after them.

It wasn't ten minutes later when Ob and Gern skidded back into the driveway carrying a small suitcase. "It was totally easy," Ob said, "he wasn't home and our mom was outside doing laundry. She didn't even know we were there."

They opened the case on the map table. The camera was a small, black metal box with a pistol-like handle. Chalo and Inder figured out how to load the film and run the camera, then they got ready for the ride.

"Hold on." Chalo got their attention. "We'll have to develop the film, it's gonna cost money. Everybody, empty your pockets."

"Aw, that's my comic book money!" Regin shouted.

"This is more important, Regin. Would you rather read about superheroes, or be a superhero?"

Regin quickly changed his mind and dumped all the change on

the table.

"Ten Evols," Chalo counted. "It should be enough."

The ride seemed faster this time. Soon they were cruising through the tunnel of trees, cautiously approaching the farm. Chalo stopped the gang behind a hedge that grew at either side of the small walkway gate. Mortimer was weeding out front with his back to them. They huddled on the roadside and Chalo whispered orders.

"Okay, Inder, you take the camera and film everything. Don't stop filming no matter what happens."

Inder nodded and took the camera. "Wait. What am I shooting?"

"The farmer, you durk! I'm gonna throw a rock at him. Make sure you get me in the picture too but only from the back."

Regin waved his hand to interrupt. His chubby face was red with the effort of riding. "But if somebody seems the film they will know it was us who threw rocks at him." They all turned to him, exasperated that he was even speaking.

"That's the idea, dipwad."

They got ready behind the hedge. Finally, Inder started the camera and stood up. Mortimer was still on all fours, patiently pulling weeds. Chalo jumped up, took careful aim, and hurled a stone at Mortimer's back. The rock sparked in the air a foot away from him and shot off to the right. Chalo grabbed Inder's shoulder and pulled him back down behind the bush.

"Did you get it?"

The skinny boy nodded.

"Right, let's go again, this time, everybody throw. Try to hit all over the place so we can see how big the shield is. Ready? Go."

They all jumped up and hurled a barrage of stones at Mortimer. The shield sparked and sent the stones flying, but Mortimer continued to work, completely unaware of the assault. Chalo ducked back down behind the hedge and everyone followed.

"Okay, that should do it, let's get out of here."

They quickly packed up the camera and rode back to Legly to get the film developed.

***

That evening, Mim made a big meal and sat them all down. All the scolding and talks were over and it was time to be a family again.

"So, what's up with you and Constable Tember?" Spence asked.

"Ooh, aren't we nosey," Mim said. "Let me ask you a question: what do you think of Mr. Tember?"

Spence thought a minute. "Well, other than he's a cop, he's okay. I mean, he's nice and all."

"He's super nice!" Shaley chimed in, "And he's always there when you need him to be."

"That's an important point, Shaley," Mim congratulated her, smiling to herself.

"And he's not scared of anybody cuz he's a police man," Maksey interjected.

"All very good observations. Who knew I had such smart children."

Maksey proudly raised her head. "Yeah, not like those dumb boys in the biker gang."

"Biker gang?" Mim repeated. "Oh, you mean the boys from the other block. Yeah, they're kind of odd. I want you kids to stay away from them. Boys that age are nothing but trouble."

"Those little shiks are definitely up to no good," Spence agreed.

"Spence! Watch your language or you'll see what happens to boys around here when they get up to no good." Mim swatted him with her napkin.

Maksey gave Shaley a look that told her they would have to keep a close eye on the biker boys from now on.

***

The next morning Constable Tember stopped by to make sure that the girls were okay.

"Oh yes, they're fine," Mim flirted. "Thank you so much for finding them for me, it really was sweet of you."

With the girl's room directly above the front door, Maksey and Shaley could hear every word through their open window.

"Just doing my job, ma'am…"

"Mim, please, call me Mim."

"Well, Mim, I'm just glad that they're home safe and sound with you. I know that's where I'd be if I was…uh…"

The girls looked at each other with gaping expressions.

"They're completely cheesing on each other!" Shaley whispered excitedly.

At the front door, Mim broke the awkward silence. "Maybe you would like to come by sometime for dinner. I'm sure the kids would love to see you again, the girls go on about how nice you are…and you are…nice, I mean."

Pal turned three shades of red. "Well, that's awfully nice of you to say, Mim, I think you're very…very nice yourself. I would love to stop by for dinner sometime. I don't get home cooked meals very often. Never really."

Upstairs, the girls had buried their heads in their pillows to keep from being heard as they giggled and screamed with a mixture of embarrassment and excitement.

As the constable left, Mim closed the front door, gave a hoot, and fanned herself. The girls came barreling down the stairs to tease their mother mercilessly.

***

Later, as steam rose from the drying pavement, the day brightened and Maksey dragged Shaley outside.

"Come on, Shaley, you're so slow!"

"Where are you going?"

"Those boys know something," Maksey said seriously. "We have to find out what."

They doubled up on Maksey's bike again with Shaley driving, and rode down the block to find the boys' hideout. The pile of tin foil covered bikes in the front yard was a dead giveaway. As they parked the bike and made their way up to the garage, Shaley held out her hand.

"Ssh, listen."

A whirring noise ran beneath a layer of chatter from the boys. They seemed to be commentating on something. There was a window in the side door, and Maksey could see through a gap in the curtain they'd pulled across it.

Shaley started to get nervous. "What are they doing?"

"Watching a movie."

Shaley had had enough. "We're gonna get in trouble. Let's go."

Reluctantly, Maksey tip-toed back to the bike. From what little Maksey had glimpsed, the boys had obviously been busy doing some spying of their own. The sisters sped away, trying their best to look nonchalant. As she sat behind Shaley on the bike, Maksey thought about her next move. One thing was certain; she sure as heck wasn't going to let her tattletale sister in on it.

That evening, as Mim lay in bed thinking about the constable, she was so distracted she didn't hear the patter of little feet in the room next door. Maksey waited until she thought her mother was asleep then slipped out of bed and into her robe. Shaley didn't stir as Maksey picked up her shoes, slipped quietly downstairs and out the front door. Sitting on the front step, she put on her shoes, then wheeled her bike quietly out into the street.

It took less than two minutes to get to the boys' clubhouse. Only one bike was left outside and a TV blared from somewhere inside. She had heard that Chalo lived alone with his father who was sick or something. No one ever saw the man and, as far as Maksey was concerned, she never wanted to. There was something scary about the place.

She went to the garage door and looked it over. The garage door opened like an oven, except upside down. She struggled with all of her strength but could only open it a couple of inches. Reaching under the door there was just enough room for her little arm to fit through. Squirming, she wedged herself into the crack as the door gave way little by little until at last there was enough room to squeeze in.

Inside it was pitch black. She stood and let her eyes adjust. She could just make out the shape of the projector when a set of car lights swept past. Instinctively she ducked but the car kept going. By the fading light she grabbed the film off of the projector and slid back outside.

Her heart was racing as she made for her bike, then she stopped. "Close the door, you ninny!" she scolded herself. She headed back and pushed on the door—it didn't budge. "Oh great!" She leaned all of her weight on the handle. Suddenly it gave way, shutting with a bang. In an instant she was back on her bike, her feet whirling like a fan as fear burned into her back.

She just knew half the neighborhood was chasing after her. What would Constable Tember think? He probably wouldn't even talk to her mom after he found out that her kids were criminals. She panicked all the way to her driveway. She felt horrible for what she had done, but it was done and now there was nothing to do but see it through.

Climbing slowly off the bike she turned around fully expecting to see the police and the boys, but the street was empty. She waited a minute. Maybe she had pedaled so fast that they were still catching up. Leaning forward, she looked down the street. Huh, she thought, looked like she had pulled it off. Suddenly she felt better. Like a mouse, she slipped back into the house, up the stairs, and into bed, tucking the film safely under her pillow. She fell asleep grinning at her cleverness.

Shaley was already up when Maksey woke. The first thing she did was reach under her pillow. The film was still there. It wasn't a dream, she really had done it.

"You went to bed with your shoes on? You durk, I'm telling Mom." Shaley ran to her mom's room as Maksey looked at her feet in horror.

"Maksey?" came Mim's voice from the room next door. "Come in here, honey."

Maksey shuffled slowly into Mim's bedroom, dejected and forlorn. "Aw, baby, did I not tuck you in last night? You had to sleep all night in your shoes, I'm so sorry!" As Mim smothered Maksey with kisses,

Shaley rolled her eyes and stomped downstairs.

Maksey breathed a sigh of relief. She would live another day. Now came the hard part. She took a breath and looked into her mom's face, ready to tell her first lie.

"Mom? I hear there's some new kids down the street my age, could I go and see if they want to play today?"

"Of course."

Maksey left the house feeling terrible. As soon as she had lied about the new kids she realized that the lie would never end. She would have to keep lying about the new kids and her mom would ask questions, then she would have to lie about what they did and, oh… It was horrible! She swore that after she had finished her plan she would tell the truth, take the punishment, and would never get involved in anything sneaky again.

With the film tucked safely away in her jacket, she pedaled into town, sticking to the side streets in case someone might see her. It was a short ride to the police station. Sergeant Bemis was the only one there.

To the Sergeant's surprise, Maksey went behind the counter, pulled up a chair at his desk, and proceeded to rattle off the whole story from the time she and Shaley followed the boys, up until the moment she came into the station. Bemis' head swam, partly from the detail of the story, but mostly because of Maksey's high-pitched prattle; it reminded him of his wife, which was why he hadn't heard a word of it.

Maksey handed over the film as proof that she wasn't lying about any of it. Sergeant Bemis smiled at her, stashed the film in his top drawer, and assured her that the police were on the case. Maksey was satisfied with his answer and, after confessing everything, left the station in a much better mood than when she had arrived.

Chapter 5

Pal Tember sat at the green light until it turned red again. Waking from his daydream he looked around to see if anyone had noticed. Traffic was light in Legly that morning and Tember's mood was even lighter. He had a severe case of Mim, and now he was trying to come up with any reason he could to stop by and see her again. Like an angel answering his prayer, Mim's little girl pulled up beside him at the light.

"Hullo, Constable Tember."

"Why hello, Maksey! What are you doing in town?"

"I was just talking to the other policeman. I gave him a movie of the aliens at the farmer's house."

Tember snapped out of his daze. "What?"

"It's proof that I'm not lying about everything." The light turned green. "Well, bye."

Maksey pedaled off, leaving Tember sitting at the light staring dumbly after her. Just as the light turned red again Tember laid on the gas, screeched the cruiser around in the middle of the intersection, and drove back to the station.

***

"We've had a level one incident."

"What's a level one incident?"

"A break in, you durk! Someone stole the film right off the

projector!" Chalo paced in front of the boys who were lined up in ranks. "As leader of this group it falls on me to make the call. This requires drastic measures. I have no choice. I'm going to have to go to the police."

"The cops? Are you sure, Chalo?" Regin asked.

"Listen, the constable seemed nice enough and we need to get that film back. That's the only thing that will make everyone take us seriously." Chalo glanced at the door leading into the house and thought about his father, sitting on the couch. The thought hardened his resolve. "I'm positive. Someone broke into our headquarters and stole our property. We have to report this to the police."

The boys just looked at each other.

"We'll have to clean up the place if the cops are going to be here," said Inder.

Chalo shook his head. "No, I'm going to them. Stay here. If I'm not back before nightfall, Inder, organize a rescue mission."

The gangly lad saluted in response. "I'm on it."

Chalo hopped on his bike and rode to the police station. He was sure that he would be interrogated, maybe even tortured, but he had to get that film back. It was the greatest discovery of the age and it belonged to the gang.

Rolling up to the station he bounded off the bike. No need to lock it, it was a police station. He strode through the doors. Best to make an impression, he thought. They weren't dealing with some kid here. He slapped the top of the counter.

"I'm here to report a robbery."

Startled, Sergeant Bemis got up from behind his desk. "What is this, kiddy day? Who are you? What robbery?"

"A movie was taken from our clubhouse. Someone broke in last night and stole it right off the projector. It's very important. You have to find it and bring the culprits to justice."

Bemis looked at the lad surprised. "You're quite articulate for a lad your age. What's your name, son?"

"My name is…"

"Chalo." Tember had just come in the door. "The kid's name is Chalo. He's the leader of a group of kids, a local bike club. He lives over on Crescent Drive, that's where their clubhouse is, in his garage."

Chalo turned red. "You got nothing on me!"

Bemis walked around the counter. "Easy, kid! Geez, what the heck is going on with the kids in this town?"

Tember stepped in. "I just saw Maksey, Mim's little girl. She told me she was here to hand in a film. I'm pretty sure she's your culprit."

"Wha…how?" Chalo stammered. The thought of a little girl getting one over on him was unthinkable.

"I said easy, kid! If I have to tell you again, I'm gonna put you in cuffs." He seemed half-serious too.

"It's okay, Sarge," said Tember. "I would be upset if a little girl got the jump on me too, but she's crafty this one. She said the film has evidence that will clear her of lying. More than anything she wants to be listened to and believed. I'm sure it wouldn't hurt of we just took a minute to watch this little film and find out what all the fuss is about."

"Nothing doing, mister, that's my film," Chalo interrupted. "Stolen property too!"

"The kid's right, Tember. It's his property, we don't have any right to what's on that film."

Chalo was starting to like the fat sergeant.

Tember sighed. "Well, you're right of course, but listen, son, it would really help us clear this whole thing up if we knew what was going on. Just let us take a look at the film and it might—"

"Sorry, I have my own plans. Just give me my movie back so I can get out of here. This place gives me the hee-bee gee-bees."

The sergeant handed the film over the counter. Chalo took it and bolted for the door without saying a word. As the door shut behind him, Bemis held up his hand to Tember.

"I don't want to hear it, not one word."

***

Chalo shouted a victory yell as he flew out of the station parking lot. He had faced the cops and won. He rode hard for the only place in town he felt safe, the comic book shop. Never in a million years had he thought he was going to get out of there not only unscathed but with the film too. Now he had to decide what to do with it.

He pulled his bike up to the store and went in, deep in thought. He wasn't showing it to the cops, that was for sure. As soon as they saw him throwing rocks at the farmer they would just throw him and the gang in jail.

Chalo perused the racks of his favorite section and tried to work it out. Who always helped the superheroes? Then his eyes came to rest on issue *#141 BugMaster*. The young man had been stung by a radio-inactive Fangamuncher and his true love, the news reporter Derla Graype , was his only connection with the normal world.

That was it! The news—they would broadcast the footage, then everyone would see the truth! There would be no way Chalo and the gang would be in trouble after everyone knew how they had cracked the case.

He ran out of the store and hopped on his bike. Swerving through traffic, he took the shortcut through the alley at Happer's clip shop and rode several blocks to the television studio. Letting his bike fall to the sidewalk, he strode in with a newly found confidence.

The secretary at the front desk looked up at him expectantly. "You're kind of young for a courier."

"I have the story of the century. You have to put this on the news." He held up the film.

"I'm sorry, unless you have an appointment with a reporter—"

"I do!" he lied.

"…and that would be?" She peered over her glasses with the kind of look that dared him to test her.

"Um…"

"With whom do you have an appointment? I need a name." She pursed her lips tightly when he didn't respond. "That's what I thought. Now leave the studio before I call the police."

Dejected, Chalo turned to go back outside. He couldn't believe it. It had gone so well at the cops just to be shut down by a snooty secretary. He got back on his bike and rode around the block, his mind churning for options.

As he turned the corner to the back of the studio, he saw a news van being unloaded by two technicians. Chalo stopped and hid behind a dumpster as the technicians pulled an equipment case through heavy, double doors. They disappeared inside as the doors slowly closed behind them. Swallowing hard, he sprinted to the doors and stuck his foot into the gap. It hurt a bit, but he stopped himself from making a sound and waited until the technicians were gone. It took all of his strength as he pried the heavy door open and slipped inside.

The hall was long and dark. Light came out through cracks in several doors before the hallway turned to the right at the end. Chalo crept along, stopping at each door. He heard the sound of talking from behind the first door. It sounded like the radio guy and someone else. His heart rose in his throat. What was he doing? The gang was right; he was being crazy.

A sudden noise caught his attention. The two technicians were coming back down the hall. Chalo searched the hall for a door. There! He spotted a door with no light coming out from under it, and dark was good for hiding. As he closed the door behind him, he heard boots walking past and breathed a sigh of relief. Out of danger for the moment, he took note of his surroundings. It looked to be some kind of small movie theater. There were several rows of chairs and a couple of stairs that led up to a projector booth. In the booth were projectors of varying sizes. One had film loaded and ready to roll and a schedule hanging on the wall.

"Afternoon executive screening. That's today. Oh shik! That's in a few minutes!"

Quickly, Chalo took the film off the projector and replaced it with his.

"That should do it." He smiled and went back down the stairs. He waited until he heard the technicians pass by as they came back into the building. Then he snuck out of the screening room, down the hall, and back outside. He was in the clear.

With a casual whistle, he walked back to his bike then rode off like a shot.

***

The sign on the desk read: Santi Shar, Advertising Manager WLEG. It was the only perk to her lousy job.

"Let's go, gentlemen. I'm sure you'll love what our producers have done for you."

The gaggle of businessmen followed her like a pack of drooling dogs. The dress was doing its job.

"Right this way." She led them down the dark hall and into the screening room. Once they were seated, she gave them the spiel. "This is the final proof for your ads. Any changes to your commercial will have to be small, text items only. No production changes, you signed off on those months ago…" Blah, blah, she thought, same old thing, and most of these guys knew the drill.

Bosco Sherf watched her carefully. The Army had spent good money on this ad and they expected results in the form of new blood. Recruiting was his command and he had put his neck on the line to convince his superiors that local television was the way to get bodies into boots.

Santi gave the order to roll film. Five minutes later, the stunned businessmen exploded into a sea of incredulous complaints. Santi leapt up the stairs to the projection room as Bosco Sherf ran for the nearest phone.

***

It had been days since Pal Tember had seen Mim. *Should I call her?* He wondered. *She'll probably think I'm stalking her.* Maybe if he discovered what Maksey was on about it would lead him to a reason to knock on Mim's door, but he needed a real reason. He didn't want to come across as desperate.

His mother had told him once, "There's nothing as unattractive as a desperate man."

Maksey's recent adventures had happened on the land outside the Townes' farm. She had claimed to see something odd, and her sister had too, even if she wasn't saying anything about it. The fact that she was keeping quiet about it made it all the more suspicious. Something had scared the poor girl and Tember was going to find out what it was.

It was his third time by the farm that day, but this time he knew as soon as he turned onto Namarin Road that something was up at Mortimer's. A car was parked in front of the hedge, out of sight of the house. As Tember got closer he could see the car was plain, too plain. A government stooge, he thought.

Sure enough, standing at the hedge was a small man in a black suit throwing rocks at Mortimer's back while the old man, mostly blind and deaf and with his back turned towards the road, shaped the bushes against the house with a power trimmer.

Tember couldn't believe his eyes—the rocks bounced off.

He slammed the brakes and stopped the cruiser in the middle of the road. The man, unaware of Tember, reached into his jacket and drew out a pistol. As he leveled it at the back of Mortimer's head, Tember ran across the road and seized the weapon. Tember easily overpowered the man, who spun around angrily.

"What do you think you're doing? You're interfering with a high level military operation. Now get out of here or I'll have your badge!"

"Sorry, mister, but around here shooting somebody is against the law. Now put your hands over your head before I start putting holes in you."

"You shik-brained country imbecile. I'm Pom Debry, Military Liaison of the Fremian Army. You mess with me and it'll be the last thing you ever wished you never did!"

Tember had no idea and didn't care. The man had pulled a gun on Mortimer after throwing rocks at the poor old man. Tember wasn't a violent man, but he'd had enough of this joker. When his fist connected with the man's flapping jaw, Debry went down like a wet sock.

***

Debry woke to a throbbing pain on the side of his face. The cell was bright and the bed hard. He sat up, angry but cautious. He didn't want another clout from that lummox of a cop.

"Well, look who's up. How do ya feel, mister army man?' Sergeant Bemis leered through the bars. "You don't look so good. Maybe you'll think twice before doing something stupid like TRYIN TA SHOOT A DEFENSELESS OLD MAN!" Bemis screamed.

It scared Debry so bad he fell off of the bed and scrambled into the corner. "You…you're all crazy! Nut cases, the lot of ya. When I get a hold of the regional commander he's gonna have a thing or two to say about how you treat army personnel."

The cell was the last of three that had been built into a short, dead end hallway off of the main office. Suddenly the hall went dark as a tall figure blocked the light. He was wearing a long coat and a wide brimmed hat. Debry could see Bemis and Tember exchange a few quiet words with the newcomer, then he came slowly down the hall.

"Major Debry." The man's voice was low and rumbled with authority. "Assault with a deadly weapon is a very serious offense, and one, I'm afraid, you're going to have to answer to."

He came up to the bars. The long dark coat, wide-brimmed hat, and grim look said it all: a Special Inquisitor. These guys had carte blanche to investigate any government service. They were like Special Forces and Internal Affairs all rolled into one.

A wave of nausea washed over Debry. What the heck was he doing here? Debry squirmed. "Look, I'm just following orders."

"Which are?" the Inquisitor inquired.

"Which are classified, although I am happy to discuss them with you in private, Inquisitor…"

"Moore, Halkus Moore is my name. Fine, we'll talk in private. Gentlemen, would you do us a courtesy?"

Tember looked at Bemis, who shrugged. "No problem, we'll be in the office." The two left, and Halkus came up close to the bars; his eyes bore into Debry like fiery knives.

"All right," he rumbled, "I'm listening."

THE SHIELDING OF MORTIMER TOWNES

Chapter 6

The boys listened, wide eyed to Chalo's story.

"No way!" one of them remarked.

"Yep, just like I said. You can call the cops and ask them yourself."

Regin was still having a hard time believing it. "And they just let you go?"

"I don't know," Chalo laughed, "when the fat sergeant handed over the film, I was outta there before they knew what was going on."

"So maybe they're still after you?" Ob said, scanning the clubhouse for a hiding place.

"Naw, they would have been here by now. I'm in the clear." Chalo crossed his arms confidently. "Besides, that film was stolen property, pure and simple. We're the good guys. Good guys don't have to worry about the law."

"One thing's for sure," Inder chimed in, "there is definitely something weird going on around here and the cops know about it."

Chalo looked at his second in command. "Inder's right. It's time to ramp up our operations. It's time for Operation Hero Watch."

The boys looked at each other and nodded.

"Cool!"

"Finally! We get to do something for real!"

Chalo produced a sheet of paper and tacked it to the wall next to the door. "This is the watch schedule. We're going all day and night. I'm first. We'll be patrolling the neighborhood from Crescent Drive to Almers Street, over to Sidel's Bakery then up to Namarin Road." He produced a pair of binoculars and held them up.

"Woah!" Gern reached for the binoculars. "Are those real?"

"Yes, Gern, and if you break them, the pain you feel will be real and it will last for a long time."

Gern withdrew his hand, suddenly not wanting anything to do with the binoculars.

"When you get to Namarin road, use these to check out the old fert's place. If there's an alien base in the area, that's got to be where it is. Our job is to find out what's going on, so report anything weird."

"Like the cops pulling up to the house?" Ob said, looking out the window of the side door.

"Yes like…what?" Chalo bolted to the side door and looked outside. "Where?" The other boys stacked around Chalo to see, but he shoved them all back. "Get offa me! Ob, you dape, there's no cops!"

"Yeah there is, over at that house." Ob pointed up the block to Mim's.

Chalo looked carefully, he could just spot the corner of the house and a piece of the driveway. Sure enough, there was a police cruiser parked out front.

"Good eyes, Ob." He nodded appreciatively.

Ob grinned, unused to such recognition.

"Okay everybody, operational note. Make sure you keep an eye on any activity, especially on that house."

***

Tember pulled the cruiser into Mim's driveway. His heart rate went up as he got out of the car and she opened the door to greet him. "Hi, Mim, you look great!"

"Aw, you're so sweet!" She blushed. She was starting to wonder why he hadn't come around in a while. She'd had just enough time to check her hair, put on a dash of lipstick, and be at the door as he arrived. "So, what brings you out this way?" This was it; he was going to ask her out. Her eyes flashed with anticipation.

"Well, actually, I'm here to talk to you about Maksey."

"Oh," she said, crestfallen.

"She's gotten herself in a bit of trouble and I—"

"Trouble? Maksey, come down here at once!" she barked.

"It's not like that, Mim, she tried to—"

Maksey scampered down the stairs but froze as soon as she saw the constable. Her wide eyes looked from him to Mim.

"Maksey, the constable is here to talk to me about some kind of trouble you've been in. Would you care to explain?"

This was not how Tember had wanted things to go. "No, Mim, really she's—"

"Constable Tember, I raise my children to tell the truth and do the right thing. The only version of events I am interested in right now is hers. Maksey?"

Tember looked apologetically at Maksey. Maksey sighed and began telling Mim the whole story, just as she had at the police station. Mim listened patiently and when Maksey was done, she looked at Tember.

"Does that about cover it?"

Tember took off his hat. "Yes, ma'am." He felt like he was the one in the hot seat.

She turned back to Maksey. "Now. How do you feel right now?"

Tears rolled down Maksey's cheeks. "Awful."

"Well, just imagine how that boy feels. You need to fix this, Maksey. Do you know how?"

"Uh-huh."

"How?"

"Tell the truth."

"That's right. Now go and get Shaley for me."

Maksey ran up the stairs as Mim turned, arms crossed, and looked at Tember. "Is that what you came here for?"

"No, Mim, not entirely. That was really impressive though. No wonder your children are so…well, amazing."

Mim shot him a look that told him he wasn't out of hot water yet.

Shaley came down and sat on the bottom stair. "Yeah Mom?"

"Shaley, did you hear what Maksey just told me?"

"No, but Spence was listening and he told me—"

"Shaley! Enough! The tattling has got to stop! You have to take responsibility for yourself and stop trying to blame things on others. I need you to keep an eye on Maksey, not to get her in trouble, but to keep her out of it."

Shaley hung her head. "Yes Mom."

***

At the top of the stairs, Spence sat and considered all he had heard. He knew Maksey was adventurous, but this was extreme even for her. He was certain that there was more to this story, and he was going to find out what it was.

***

Tember drove Maksey and Mim down the block to Chalo's house and parked the cruiser at the curb. The boys watched from the open garage, not knowing what to do. Maksey marched up to the front door with Mim and rang the bell.

Ob was about to say something, but Inder smacked him on the

back of the head.

Maksey rang again. Finally, the door opened.

Chalo's father, Wane, was a thin man in every way. Thin hair, thin beard, thin build, and thin brain. He eyeballed Tember watching him from the cruiser, then took an unhealthy look at Mim. Up and down he surveyed, his mouth parting slightly as he filled his gaze.

"Mister..." she began.

"Wane. What d'you two want?" He glared at Maksey, then went back to scanning Mim.

"This is my daughter Maksey. She is here to apologize to you and your son."

"BOY! In. Now!"

Chalo came to the door, slightly shaken. "Yessir?"

"You know this one?"

"Yessir."

"Go on then, girl."

Maksey looked Chalo in the eye. "I'm sorry I took your..." she looked at Wane who was busy checking out Mim, "...things. I promise never to ever take anything as long as I live."

Chalo, impressed by Maksey but clearly more worried about his father than anything else, stuck out his hand. "No problem."

Maksey took it and gave a firm shake. Chalo scratched the inside of her palm and rolled his eyes towards the garage. Maksey nodded.

"Chalo," said Mim, "please tell Maksey that what she saw was just a movie trick and not actually real."

Chalo shrugged and said, "Yeah, it's really fake, nothing but fake...movie stuff."

"There, see?" Mim reassured her.

Maksey just looked at her with a big smile.

Wane glowered at Maksey. "Is that it?"

Mim stepped in. "That is it. I apologize for any inconvenience."

"Oh, it's no bother. You can inconvenience me anytime."

"Goodbye." Mim turned on her heels with Maksey in tow and headed back to the police cruiser.

Maksey looked back at Chalo who quickly pointed a finger to the clubhouse. Maksey grinned to herself. She was in.

"Well, how did it go?" Tember asked as they climbed back into the cruiser.

"Maksey was an angel, Chalo was a gentleman, but his father. What a piece of work!"

"Was he rude to you? I'll go back and—"

"No, Pal, forget it. He's not worth it."

Back at Mim's house, they pulled into the driveway and she thanked Tember for bringing this to her attention.

"Would you like to come in for a hot cup of—"

"I have to get back to the station, but if it's all right with you, I'd love to stop by later, maybe for dinner?"

***

Maksey watched her mom and Officer Tember with a strange fascination, then snapped out of it, remembering that Chalo and his gang were waiting. "Mom, I'm gonna go play at my new friend's house." There was that lie again. She winced.

"Okay, that's fine, sweetie." Her mom turned her attention back to Officer Tember. "Oh, that would be so nice. And afterwards we can look at the stars from the back porch. The view is great from back there."

"The view is just fine from right here," Tember murmured, then seemed to shake himself awake. "I uh…really should get going."

"I'll see you tonight then?"

"Count on it."

Ew, Maksey thought as she backed away from the two adults. She picked up her bike off the front lawn but then hesitated. She really didn't want to go back and face all those older boys alone. She would need Shaley. Shaley had always been close with Maksey, but lately she was starting to find reasons not to hang out with her. She was more interested in listening to records or going to the movies with friends from school. Problem was, their neighborhood wasn't close to any of Shaley's friends, so Shaley had to get Mim to drive her or arrange a sleepover. Shaley had been on a lot of sleepovers lately, and Maksey was beginning to feel left out. Maybe if Shaley would come with her, she would realize how exciting Maksey's life was right now and would want to do more with her.

***

Maksey tossed a pebble against hers and Shaley's bedroom window. "Shaley!" she hissed.

The window opened. "What?"

"Come on!" She gave her sister an urgent look.

Shaley turned down the record player in their room then came back to the window. "What are you freaking out about?"

"I need your help!" Maksey's head went a little dizzy from whispering so loudly.

Rolling her eyes, Shaley shouted, "You're such a pain in the butt! What do you want?"

"Shhh! Come on, they're waiting!"

"Who's waiting? What are you talking about?"

Maksey pointed down the street.

"You little…are you going back to those boys' house?"

"Shhh! Mom will hear. Just come on!"

Shaley thought a minute—babysitting Maksey again, not her idea of fun. But then maybe going to a house full of boys slightly older than her wouldn't be so bad after all.

"Okay, I'll take you this once."

She clomped down the stairs and out the front door, banging soundly.

"Be quiet!" Maksey said, exasperated.

Shaley climbed onto the bike in front of Maksey. "Oh, calm down. Mom is in the kitchen. I think she's gaga over Officer Tember. She's cooking half the kitchen for dinner." She stood on the pedals and they headed off down the street.

***

Chalo's garage door was closed, but Ob came out as soon as the girls pulled up.

"We were expecting you, but not you." He looked from Maksey to Shaley.

"She's my sister. Where I go, she goes." Maksey folded her arms like she meant business. "Besides, she knows everything."

Shaley was suddenly aware that, for the first time, one of her siblings was actually sticking up for her. "Yeah, where she goes, I go."

Ob, convinced by their sheer confidence, just shrugged, "Okay," and led them inside.

The boys leapt to their feet. Chalo had already briefed them on what had happened, and had even rehearsed his lines; they were straight out of one of his favorite movies.

"So, you thought you would return to the scene of the crime, eh?"

Maksey looked at him confused. "You told me to."

"It's okay, while you're here you're under my protection. No one will lay a finger on ya or they answer to me, and I only answer questions one way. With a bullet to the guts." Chalo struck a gangster pose and made machine gun noises.

"Ooo-kay." Shaley looked at him like he was kooky.

"I'm just kidding, I always wanted to say that. Welcome to the secret lair of the Crescent Street…um, superhero club, thing, whatever. All of us, in one way or another, are involved in defending this neighborhood from the forces of evil."

"Yeah, on a daily basis," Inder added.

"You mean annoying the neighborhood on a daily basis," Shaley quipped.

"Ah, a skeptic. That's good, we need one of those," Inder retorted.

"Well," Maksey spoke up, "why did you want me to come back?"

"Cuz you're the only one outside our club to see the shield."

"The what?"

"The invisible shield around the old farmer. You saw it, right?"

Maksey nodded.

"Yeah, and we saw the snake-man rising into the sky, so we went into the woods to look for his hiding place," Shaley blurted, wanting to get one up on the boys.

Maksey elbowed her.

"What snake-man?"

The boys all crowded around the girls.

"What was he like?"

"Did he have a gun?"

"Easy lads." Chalo stepped in. "Give 'em some space." He had heard that girls spook easily. "Maybe our guests would like a seat?" Chalo took Shaley by the arm and walked her over to the old couch. "Ob, Gern, bring them a couple of sodas."

Ob and Gern raced off to their house to fetch the drinks.

Chalo sat on the arm of the battered old couch. "Now, tell us about what you saw."

It took about thirty minutes before the whole story was told. Maksey left nothing out and Shaley filled in her part as well. Maksey wondered why Shaley was so willing to tell all when she had pretended not to know anything in front of their mom. She was acting weird, and Chalo seemed to be directing all of his attention towards her instead, which was starting to tick Maksey off. Didn't these boys realize there was something serious going on?

"Well, our next step is clear. Go interrogate the old man."

"What do you mean?" Maksey asked.

"It means we have to talk to him and ask him what is going on. He'll know that his cover is blown so there's no telling what he'll do. He may even try to kill us."

"Mister Townes would never! He's really nice. He would never hurt anybody ever!" Maksey objected loudly.

"Okay, kid, geez. If you like the old guy so much, you talk to him."

Chapter 7

The walls of the cell were black, dry, and seamless. Ilgut's skin chaffed as he writhed against the restraints.

"Sure, keep at it. You can squirm all day. I never get tired of watching you in misery. Of course, you can just tell me who hired you for this hit and I can give you a nice, steamy cell with a bed of Nytarian moss. Sound good?"

"Chugtang, you old washed up old dahjkak. Your tactics are feeble. I'm a professional, I never divulge my sources."

"Professional what, Ilgut? Loser? Yeah, I'll agree with that, but hit man? I've never seen a poorer excuse for an assassin than you. You should really change your line of work…oh, but I think you just did. Now you're going to be a professional icebreaker. We'll make sure it's on a nice, dry planet, with lots of frozen water and none of those pesky bugs you like to call dinner.
"You called me a dahjkak, let's see, that translates to 'dry skin' if I'm correct? Well, you're right. I have dry skin AND lots of fur, so cold doesn't bother me. Does it bother you? 'Cause I'm going to visit you all the time just to torment you for the rest of your stinking life! Now, tell me who hired you!"

Ilgut just squirmed against his bonds and said nothing.

Chugtang was at his wits end. "Get this bug sucker out of my sight."

The guards triggered the eHarness, freezing Ilgut with a painful electrostatic shock, and hauled him out of the room.

As a senior agent, Chugtang had seen so many hardened crooks like this that he'd lost count, so Ilgut knew his threats were very real.

When the UGPo (Unified Galactic Police) put someone away, they were very thorough. Chugtang admired Ilgut for not being a snitch but there had to be a thread somewhere, something that would lead to the next bad guy further up the chain.

"Sir?" One of Chugtang's researchers came over his SynapsiCom.

"What is it, Tarker?"

"We've got a hit on the planetary registry."

"Show me."

Though nothing changed in the room, to Chugtang's eyes the walls filled with information, all manipulated by his thoughts.

"The planetary registry doesn't list the claimant sir, but it was filed by a legal representative in sector one-five two-five. A licensed galactic business attorney by the name of Drom –"

"Drom Slymbal, I know him. He's a worm. Bring him in."

***

Red clouds gave way to a deepening purple sky as the stars winked in one by one. Mortimer and Aga took their dinner in the sitting room and watched the news as they did every evening of the long years they had been together. Unaware of the adoring old couple, the news anchor droned the events of the day.

"Today, the Fremian Leadership Counsel formally accused the Republic of Olred of developing weapons of mass defense in the form of a high altitude anti-aircraft system. The system is reported to use a series of manned, high altitude balloons equipped with machine guns to shoot down any planes that enter Olred airspace. In response to the allegations, Olred has in turn formally accused Fremia of making accusations in order to cover up Fremian weapons of mass defense programs that are, quote, undoubtedly going on, unquote.

"Furthermore, the leader of the Republic of Olred had this to say…"

On the TV, the Olred leader came on looking tired and slightly peeved. "The truth will always come out, and when it does, Fremia will be left holding their bags!"

"More now from Barv Tweezman, our foreign allegory interpreter…"

***

"Okay, Sarge, I'm back. Anything out of our trigger-happy-nut-job?"

"Nope, quiet as a tomb."

"Where's the Inquisitor?"

"He's still in there."

"What? All this time? What the heck is he doing in there?" Tember looked down the hall. He could see Halkus leaning up against the bars saying something to Debry. Suddenly the big man stood and came back up the hallway.

"Let him go."

Bemis' jaw fell open mid-chew on a cherry-glazed cruller

Tember was incredulous. "No way, I caught this guy red handed trying to shoot an innocent civilian."

Halkus held up his hands. "I know, I know, by all rights he should be locked away for a long time, but Debry is a military liaison and if you guys have been following the news, then you know that things are a bit tense right now."

"No, no, no!" Bemis wiped his red face and stomped towards the Inquisitor. "We caught him and he's not leaving that cell."

"Listen, I understand, believe me. Look, I'll let you in on a little information. We're about a gnats breath away from war with Olred right now, and a big part of it has very much to do with this little town of yours. Legly is about to become the military epicenter of the Fremian continent. So, like it or not, you have to stand down."

Debry emerged from the hallway.

Bemis looked at him in shock. "How did you…?"

"I let him out." Halkus held up a large ring full of keys.

"Inquisitor privilege. They're all master keys." He followed Debry to the door where he stopped and looked back. "One more thing. You gentlemen might want to look into getting new digs. There are a lot more changes on the way."

Tember watched in disbelief as Halkus and Debry left. "How do ya like that? Just waltzes in and takes our prisoner."

Bemis sat down and reached for another donut, changed his mind, and threw the box in the trash. Tember tried to fit together the pieces of the puzzle that he had so far. Mim, Maksey, Chalo, Debry, Halkus, and in the middle was Mortimer Townes and whatever heavenly forces were protecting him. There were still a lot of pieces missing.

"Things are getting weird around here and I have the feeling that it's only the beginning. I think we should take the Inquisitor's advice. If the military moves in they could commandeer our weapons, vehicles, records—everything."

Bemis looked at him with a grim face. "It appears our Inquisitor was trying to do us a favor, let's not let it go to waste."

***

Outside the station Halkus threw Debry his car keys. "Here ya go, you're free as a bird. Just make sure you don't fly off the handle."

"Shikhead," Debry muttered, and drove off, checking in the mirrors to make sure Halkus wasn't tailing him. He muttered all the way to his motel.

Up in his room he poured himself a drink, picked up the phone, and dialed a long series of numbers.

"Debry. Password: Bags. It works. Yeah, it stopped all the rocks. I don't know how strong it really is. Yeah, I suppose we could ramp it up. What are you thinking? DynoBlast? Okay, it's gonna draw attention though. What's that? Stump removal? I like it."

***

Special Inquisitor Halkus Moore parked his long, black cruiser next to the phone booth across the road from Debry's motel. His eyes never left the motel as he got out of the car and entered the booth. He dialed quickly, only four digits.

"Agency clearance required," a woman's voice intoned.

"Moore, one nine seven four. You got my report?"

"Yes, sir, wait one…" There was a click, a pause, and then…

"Moore? Chief here. This Townes guy is too clean. Seems he's never done anything but work his farm and go to church."

"I've been on him a couple of days now. It appears he is completely unaware of the attacks. I think he's legit. People like that actually do exist you know."

"Okay, Halkus, I trust your judgment. Could it be that the military is testing something on him, you know, using him like some kind of winnie-pig?"

"That's really sick, but it's exactly their style and Debry is just the stooge to do it. I need more evidence though."

"Get it then, and put this thing to bed."

Halkus hung up the phone just in time to see Debry's boxy, olive green staff car pull out of the motel parking lot.

***

It was difficult for Tember to shake off the feeling that the shik was about to hit the fan, but he was determined to put aside his concerns and just enjoy the evening with Mim and her children. Checking his hair one last time, he pulled his police cruiser into the driveway and tried to calm his heartbeat. It had been a long time since he'd been on a date. Mim was at the door to greet him in a light summer dress that clung to her in all the right places.

"Who are you and what have you done to Constable Tember?" Her smile lit up the evening.

"That's right, you've never seen me out of uniform. Well, I sent the constable home for the evening. I'm Pal, his charming sidekick, and the brains behind the dashing duo. These are for you." He handed a bouquet of flowers to her and they went inside.

During dinner, the children had all kinds of questions about being a policeman, so much so that Mim had to tell them to leave him alone and let him eat.

"When I grow up I'm gonna be a police man," Maksey said, picking at her plate.

"I think you would make a better police woman," Tember teased. "But seriously, Maksey, if you really want that, I think you have the makings of a fine police officer."

"Really?"

"Oh, definitely. You have a passion for the truth and a wonderful sense of adventure. I quite admire you for it."

"But what if you tell the truth and nobody believes you?" She looked at him earnestly.

"Well, you have to stick to your guns. The truth is the truth and that's that. It will always win out."

"But I saw the snake-man flying into the sky and nobody believes me." Her face scrunched up. "Did you ever know something that was important but no one would believe you?"

Tember set down his fork and looked at Maksey somberly. "No, Maksey, quite the opposite; I wanted to believe somebody and they let me down."

Maksey looked sad for him, but a sudden knock at the door broke the uncomfortable silence.

"I'll get it." Maksey was gone like a shot, trotting off to the front door.

"No, Maksey, I'll get it." Mim was right behind her, but when the door swung open she was surprised to see a stocky man in a black suit holding up government ID.

"Agent Debry, ma'am, Fremian Military Liaison. I'm here to interview the children about what they saw out at the Townes' farm."

"See, Mom! I told you I was telling the truth!" Maksey jumped for joy.

"Maksey, not now. Go back to the table." She pushed Maksey behind her. "I'm sorry, Mister…"

"Debry, ma'am, Agent Debry," he said sternly.

"Yes, Agent Debry. I'm sorry but we're eating dinner right now and my children have already told the local police everything they know."

"Yes, I have talked to local law enforcement." He turned and eyed the cruiser. "They have no jurisdiction in this case. I'm sorry if the time is inconvenient, but this is an important matter of Fremian military security and I'm going to have to insist." He stuck his foot into the door and began pushing it open.

"Hey! You can't come into my house!" Mim pushed back but the little man was strong. Mim was losing ground. Then Tember was there, wedging himself between Mim and the door.

"Back off, Debry, or do I have to add breaking and entering to the charges against you?"

"Constable Tember, I should have known." Debry took a step back outside and glared at Tember, towering over him. "Well, isn't this cozy, the local cop in bed with a top suspect."

"We were not in bed!" Mim spat under Pal's arm. "And just you watch your language around my children!"

"Unless you have all the right paperwork and a child consultation specialist, you're not talking to anybody, Debry." Tember came out the door and began bearing down on him. "Now I'm only telling you this once more, back off."

Debry's face turned beet red and his hand twitched for his gun, but he turned and stomped back to the car. "I'll be back, you can count on it!" The tires of the boxy little car gave a little squeak and the engine sputtered, then whined as he sped up the street.

"You okay?" Tember turned to Mim who flew out the door and wrapped her arms around him.

"Yes, thanks to you we are."

Maksey came out and joined in the hug, while Shaley and

Spence stood in the doorway.

"You scared the shik out of that guy." Spence nodded his approval.

"You watch your language, young man." Mim shot him a cool warning glare.

"Sorry, Mom."

They all returned to the table and Mim dished out extra big slices of pie to celebrate their victory, but Tember was less enthusiastic.

"He wasn't kidding, Mim. Debry will be back, and with everything he needs to interview the kids. You should prepare yourself."

"Oh, Pal, what can he do really? Some trumped up little army clown isn't going to scare me."

"Mim, you don't understand, he's not just a soldier, he's a liaison. That means he reports directly to the Fremian Counsel. This guy is top brass. I don't know what's going on but it's serious. There's not much more I can do to protect you and your family when he comes back, and he will."

***

The next morning, Maksey woke her sister up early and headed down to the clubhouse. It was time to go and talk to Mortimer face to face. Shaley complained at first but then Maksey reminded her that Chalo was going to be there. Suddenly Shaley was a flurry of activity, eager to get going.

When they arrived at the clubhouse, Chalo was alone and waiting for them. He issued them each a canteen and a candy bar, then reviewed the route on the model map. Shaley thought he was like some kind of brave rebel leader or secret agent.

"We already know how to get there. Let's go." Maksey's patience was wearing thin from all the bravado.

Chalo produced a third bike. "Here, Shaley, I got this for you."

"Really?"

"Yeah, it's Inder's but he won't mind if you use it this once."

"Thanks." Shaley blushed and they all pedaled off into the cool morning.

Chapter 8

Debry fumed all night in his motel room, but as the next day broke, he was too busy to think about his frustrations. It was nine sharp and a field agent dressed as a motel maid dropped off his uniform. He changed quickly, then climbed into the bottom of the covered maid cart for his ride down to street level. He chuckled to himself at the thought of the Inquisitor watching the empty motel room all day. As the cart wheeled past a parked van, he made the switch. The van, a Vangs County Utility vehicle, drove off with Debry in the back.

It made the turn onto Namarin Road and slowed just past the Townes' farm, parking on the road close to a large old tree. Debry and his two-man crew set to work immediately. The first thing to go were the branches as, piece by magnificent piece, the grand old tree was hacked to bits. Soon enough Mortimer appeared, chugging along in an old tractor as he prepared the fields for the season's hay.

Debry timed it perfectly as the main trunk of the huge old tree teetered slowly, then came crashing down on Mortimer as he passed. The shield held and protected not just Mortimer, but the tractor as well.

In the van a camera rolled, capturing the whole event. As the tractor ambled by, Mortimer waved and the two men with Debry feebly waved back.

"Enough gawking, you two!" Debry barked. "We have to prepare that charge by the time he comes around again."

The men ran back to the van, each taking the handle of a large wooden box marked 'DynoBlast'. They left it with Debry, then set to work clearing the felled tree with chainsaws. Soon a pile of wood covered the DynoBlast box, and a detonator line led from its hiding place back to the van, buried out of sight.

"Perfect timing," Debry said, as the tractor came lumbering back over the gentle slope of the field. He covered the last of the wire, then set out a pitcher of lemonade on top of the wood pile. "That ought to bring him in; old men love lemonade."

Debry retreated back to the van to watch. One of the crew men looked at him.

"Boss, do you *really* think that will work? I mean, it's not like he's an animal or something."

"Shut it, shikweed. I'm running this mission."

Mortimer's tractor came within a meter of the wood pile but he didn't seem to take notice of it, let alone decide to take the bait.

"Dammit! Ah well, close enough." Debry pressed the button on the detonator. Dirt and wood was thrown several hundred feet into the air. The shockwave pummeled the van, nearly tipping it over and making a sound that could be heard for miles. Chunks of dirt and pieces of wood rained down as Debry climbed out of the van and peered through the smoke.

Mortimer and his tractor trundled away, completely oblivious to the event.

"Look, boss!" The field agent pointed at the three meter-wide crater. Next to it, with a set of tractor tracks running through the middle, was a spherical impression where the soil had been blown up against the shield.

A kilometer down the road, Special Inquisitor Halkus Moore cursed as he watched through his binoculars. Suddenly, he spied three kids approaching the farm on bikes. They had stopped and were pointing at the van and the blast area.

Halkus tensed, knowing Debry was capable of anything, but thankfully the agent quickly packed up the van and drove away as the kids approached Mortimer on the tractor. They talked for a minute, then rode on the tractor with the old man up to the tree and began helping him pick up the branches and pieces of wood everywhere. Halkus was impressed with the kids' gesture, and it made him even angrier at Debry as he fired up his long black cruiser and roared off down the road after him.

***

Tired and sore, Maksey, Shaley, and Chalo returned to the clubhouse just after midday. The boys were there to meet them with grim faces. Inder stood in front, arms folded. Chalo looked him up and down.

"What gives?"

"Exactly. What gives? Why'd you take off to ride with a couple of girls?"

"Yeah." Regin stepped up and folded his arms too. "And why did you give Inder's bike to her?"

"It's not your bike, Chalo." Inder was giving his best angry face.

Maksey and Shaley just looked at each other and shrugged.

Chalo squared up to the gang. "Fair questions, every one. If you back off the attitude," he poked a finger at Inder and Regin, who both flinched and stepped back, "I'll tell you the whole story."

Ob and Gern nodded, while Inder and Regin looked at each other, their resolve crumbling. Chalo just walked into the garage and sat down on the couch, Shaley following close behind. Maksey climbed up onto the workbench and went to work on her candy bar.

"First off, it's my watch, so it's my call. I decided that the mission was necessary. It required only three people. Me as the duty watchman, Maksey as the…talker person who was gonna talk to the farmer, and her sister to back her and me up. Second, we needed the bike. Three people on two bikes is too slow. The Crescent Street bike—superhero, gang, whatever we're called—is not slow, ever. So in the interest of safety, strategy, security, reputation and…" he looked at Shaley with a grin, "…looking good, I took the initiative. I knew, or at least I thought I did, that my second in command, our executive officer, would have my back."

Inder was satisfied. "And he does, as always."

Chalo, confident he had the gang back on his side, told the whole story. The boys had, like everyone in town, heard the explosion. Mortimer brushed aside any of the children's explanations about bombs and such, but was so grateful for their help in cleaning up the branches that he gave them five Evols and congratulated them for being such good neighbors. He was very happy that the nice road crew had left him so much firewood, though he thought it was a shame that lightning had struck the old tree.

When Chalo finished his story, Inder raised his hand to make a formal proposal.

"Because they have successfully completed a mission and shown courage in the face of danger, I propose that the ban on girls be lifted, and Maksey and Shaley be made honorary members of the gang."

Chalo seconded this and the rest of the boys agreed. Shaley rode behind Chalo when he took her home to get her broken bike, while the rest of them covered Maksey's bike in tin foil. Shaley and Chalo got back just as they were finishing.

Maksey beamed as she looked over her bike. "Cool, but why do you cover it in foil?"

"To keep the aliens from knowing our location."

"Yeah, and our whereabouts."

Regin elbowed Gern. "You dape, they're the same thing."

They put Shaley's bike into the clamp on the workbench, and within an hour the bike was fixed and covered in foil. Shaley was so grateful, she hugged Chalo and shook everyone else's hand.

***

"Drom Slymbal. I gotta tell ya, Drom, it's not looking good. You've got a class two disclosure infringement and what's shaping up to be class one planet tampering. That's life times fifty. How do you think a meat roll like you is going to do in a life-level lockup?"

"Your threats only belie the fact that you have no proof with which to procure incarceration. You are wasting my time, as well as yours, which you should be spending trying to get a confession out of your suspect."

"Nah, he lacks motive. Ilgut's never done anything he wasn't getting paid to do. Besides, he really doesn't have the brains for anything on this scale. But you, you're a different story."

"So you have determined that it takes a certain amount of intellect to fly down to a planet and shoot at one of the natives? It seems to me that stupidity is the prime requisite for such a foolish act. The simplest answer is usually the correct one, and certainly this case is no exception. I am confident, especially when it comes to a jury, that such a point will be painfully obvious."

Chugtang nodded at his intern. The room went dark as aerial footage of Ilgut's attack on Mortimer played on the wall. It was the second time Chugtang had seen it. He watched Drom's reaction as the footage rolled, but the slug was stoic. Suddenly, out of the corner of his eye, he spotted something in the video.

"Again," he told his intern. "Get used to seeing this, Slymbal," he said, masking his excitement. "They'll be playing this a lot at the trial."

Chugtang scanned the footage as it finished, then turned the lights back on and looked at his intern, who shook his head. They still hadn't got approval to release the identity of the claim owner.

"For now, Slymbal, you're free, but don't go anywhere. When I get the little bit of data that I'm waiting for, I'm confident, especially when it comes to a jury, that you're going to be put away for life times fifty."

He stormed out of the room and slammed the door but it was all a show. His intern was on his heels.

"Screening room, now!" Chugtang barked. They turned the corner and went into a small, barren room. "Get me the chief." The intern quickly put through the call. "Chief, Chugtang. I've got something you need to see."

"Not right now…"

"Tam-Tam Chief." He spoke in code.

"Two ticks… Okay, Chugtang, what have you got?"

Chugtang nodded at the intern, who rolled the footage again so the chief could see it on screen through the video call.

"Stop…there," Chugtang ordered.

The footage froze. In the corner of the shot were two little girls pointing at Ilgut as the tractor beam dragged him up into the atmosphere. Chugtang turned the lights back on. On the comm, the chief slapped his forehead.

"They saw him. We've got a contamination."

***

That evening, Mortimer finished repairing several windows that had broken on one side of the house. Tired from a long day's work, he settled into his chair as Aga brought in their meal. After a prayer of thanks, he turned up the TV.
"Tonight: the incredible footage that reveals Olred spies using Fremian civilians as test subjects for a dangerous new technology."

***

That same evening, in another house, Tember was enjoying dinner with Mim and the kids again. They had just finished and sat down to watch some TV when the breaking news story flashed onto their screen. Chalo's footage played, showing the rocks bouncing off of Mortimer's back.
Maksey jumped up. "Where are the boys? The real one shows the boys throwing the rocks."

Mim looked from Maksey to Tember. "What is this? That looks like Mr. Townes."

Tember touched Mim on the arm. "This is what it looks like when the shik hits the fan."

On the news, the anchor intoned somberly, "Fremia has cut all diplomatic ties to Olred, with the Fremian Leadership Counsel declaring an official state of inhospitable posturing towards the Olred Republic. Olred has responded to the declaration by doubling the number of anti-aircraft balloon emplacements."

***

The Fremian forces came first by air, hovering around the perimeter of the farm. Then came the ground forces. They blocked

Namarin Road and set up headquarters at the stump of the old tree. Scouts were sent to the house but they couldn't make it past the shield, which had expanded to protect most of the property, including several acres of fields. Teams of scientists set up equipment at the shield's edge to test it as Debry paced in front of the stump, which now served as a table in his sprawling, olive green command tent.

He needed answers, any answers would do. Answers got rewards, no answers got…he didn't want to think about it. He had teams at the police station, the town hall, and at every suspect's residence. He would get those answers, even if he had to make them up.

As Debry paced and planned, a shadow darkened the door to his command tent.
"Quite a show, Debry."

"Inquisitor Moore, still lurking about? This is all your fault, you know. If you had done your job, you would have seen what Olred was up to. But no, the big ball of incompetence is always built by others, and eventually rolls to the door of the military, who has to pick it up and clean up the mess. You never learn, you people. Plan diligently, act decisively, that is how you get things done. THAT is real power. That is also why I will claim the glory while you quietly retire in shame."

"You may see power and glory, Debry, but I see a ball dropping, and it's dropping right on your head. The nice part is, I'll be right there when it does."

Debry snatched his coat off the stump and stormed out. "Driver!" Debry barked.

A soldier held open his car door. Debry ducked into the vehicle and sped away.

Halkus followed.

***

Mim smiled drowsily as the morning breeze blew into her open bedroom window. She had just woken up from a dream where the girls had climbed into bed with her. She could see their sleeping faces and wondered who was hammering downstairs.
Her mind snapped awake and she scrambled into her robe. "Coming!" She pulled on her slipper, hopping out the bedroom as the

hammering continued. "I said I'm coming, hold your horses! Geez."

Reaching the front door, she snatched it open, ready to unleash a torrent of scolding, but nothing came out as she faced over forty combat ready soldiers with Debry's sneering grin in the lead. A helicopter thumped through the sky overhead and a tank had its turret cannon leveled directly at her head.

A bird croaked in the distance, and Debry leaned forward slightly. "I told you I'd be back."

The soldiers stormed into the house and dragged Mim into the girls' room. Outside, a scaffold was erected and a crew began to cover the house in huge olive green tarps. In the adjoining house, the neighbors closed the curtains and pretended they weren't home. Mim was blindfolded, handcuffed, gagged, and stuffed into one of the girls' little chairs. When the blindfold was lifted, all she could see was a light bulb shining into her face as she struggled against her bonds.

"It's no use resisting. You're in a lot of trouble, lady."
A soldier removed the gag.

"You people are demented! You –"

"That's enough of that!" Debry's face came inches away from her own, as he held a gun up to her head and pulled back the hammer. "It's come down to this: you forced my hand and now you are the subject of a top level military interrogation and—"

"No, I'm in my little girls' room with their reading lamp pointed at my face which, by the way, you better be careful with, or I'll have them take it out of your salary." Mim was unfazed. "Does your mother know what you're doing right now? I bet if she did, she would be very upset with you."

"Fine, if you won't talk, maybe your children will."

"You leave them out of this!" Mim yelled, straining against her bonds again.

"Wilkins, get me the girls," Debry sneered.

"Yes, sir."

"After all, Mim, it all started with them, didn't it? You pretended not to believe them when they told you about spies in your own backyard, because you were helping those spies. Now, your own children will be the ones who put you behind bars."

"Sir?"

"What, Wilkins, where are the girls?"

"Gone, sir."

Chapter 9

Chalo watched the patrolling army helicopter disappear over the ridge of trees through his binoculars. "Okay, it's gone," he said.

The boys all huddled in the garage looking nervous.

"You all look like a bunch of scared dapes. The army has Maksey and Shaley and it's our duty to get them back. After all, they're part of the club…gang…whatever. This is what we've been waiting for, a real adventure!"

Chalo cleared the comics off the top of an old travel trunk that served as a coffee table, and reached inside. He handed out colored bed sheets, one color for each member.

"It's time to be what you were meant to be." He held up a pair of scissors. "Real heroes."

***

One by one they went. Bemis watched helplessly as his donuts disappeared. The soldiers just grinned at him as they wiped the glaze from their faces. Tember leaned against the wall as the soldiers milled about the room, going through drawers, cabinets, and shelves. Halkus had been right; it was a full takeover.

As Sergeant Bemis watched the last of his donuts go down a soldier's throat, he decided he'd had enough. He got Tember's attention and discreetly motioned for the man to call his desk phone. It took Tember a second to figure out the Sergeant's sign language but eventually he got it.

Tember inched over to his own desk and unhooked the phone from the receiver just slightly. Then he quickly dialed the single digit to ring Bemis' desk. A soldier reached for the ringing phone but Bemis lunged and got it first.

"Legly Police desk. Oh, hello, Mrs. Jenkins. What's that? Again? It's not really a good day for this, Mrs. Jenkins, did you try your neighbor? Too afraid of the soldiers to go outside you say?"

Tember gave him an exasperated look.

"Oh, okay, we'll be right over." Bemis hung up the phone. "Tember, Mrs. Jenkins' grat is up the tree again. Let's go." They both grabbed their gear and headed for the door.

"Wait a minute you two." They froze as a large soldier barred their way. "No weapons." Before they could comply, a couple of soldiers removed their pistols for them. "Okay, you can go."

They quickly stepped out the door and climbed into Tember's police cruiser.

"Jenkins' grat? Is that the best you could come up with?"

"Well, I thought grats like fish and fish stink, and something stinks around here."

"Where did you get your cop license, a pet store? So, where are we going?"

Bemis cranked the old cruiser to life. "Your girlfriend's house."

"Mim? She's not my—"

"Whatever, her kids have something to do with all of this, so we start there." Tember wasn't going to argue, it was where he wanted to go anyway.

***

It was a short ride up the street. They stashed their bikes in a hedge behind someone's house, then worked their way through the row of back gardens until they were on the other side of Mim's garden fence. The soldiers had quickly installed the huge canvas that covered the house, and the scaffolding was still in place.

"Now what?" Inder asked.

"Issue three." Chalo smiled.

"What? What is he talking about?" Regin was sweating profusely.

A grin grew on Inder's face. "Issue three of DynaMan, you dape. He's not in his suit, but he rescues Natamie from her penthouse using the sheets from the clothes line."

Regin frowned. "But we don't have a clothes line full of sheet—" Chalo reached over the boy's shoulder and held the cape Regin was wearing to his face. "Oh."

Chalo volunteered to go up the scaffold because, he argued, he was the only one who was in black and he would be camouflaged against the olive green tarp. In truth, the other boys were glad they weren't picked to do the climbing and happily took up the duty of causing a distraction.

The climb was quick and easy up the scaffold to the roof. Chalo scrambled up the tiles to the peak. Down on the street, Ob, Gern, and Inder climbed all over the tank. The soldiers rushed to try and get the boys down, but they were too fast to get caught. By then, Chalo had crept down the front of the roof and lowered himself to the scaffold outside the girl's window.

He quietly slipped behind the canvas and was about to tap on the glass when he heard the sound of adults talking. Peering over the edge of the window, he saw Debry interrogating Mim. He ducked back down, his heart racing. Where were the girls?

Down in the street, the soldiers had caught Ob and Gern, but Inder was still giving them a chase.

Chalo went to the next window; Mim's empty bedroom. He couldn't believe his luck, the window was open. He slid in and went to the door.

He could still hear the interrogation going on in the next room but no sound in the hall. He risked a peek out the door—all clear. He opened the door a little more and looked around. The door to Spence's room was open at the end of the hall. Just inside, Chalo could see a small closet that used to be part of the main hall before being remodeled, now on the far side of Spence's room.

Suddenly, the closet door bumped open to reveal a laundry chute and a pair of upside-down feet kicking in the air. Chalo sprinted quietly down the hall. It was Shaley, trying to go head first down the chute. As he grabbed her legs, she started to scream.

"No, shh! Shaley, it's me, Chalo! I'm here to rescue you!"

Shaley looked up at him through the chute. "Chalo? Are you crazy? What are you doing here?"

Chalo heard Debry call for a soldier and knew that someone was going to come out of that door soon. "No time! Sorry." He pushed Shaley down the chute and followed after. They landed in a pile of laundry in the basement.

"Are you okay?" Chalo helped her up. Shaley lunged at him with a hug.

"Nice outfit." Shaley admired his superhero costume.

"Can we go now, you two?" said Maksey, who had already gone down the chute ahead of her sister.

"How do we get out of here?" Chalo looked around.

Shaley went over to a small window up high in the back wall. "Ta da."

Chalo went first, because he was dressed in black, and gave the all clear for the girls. They were up and over the fence before anyone was the wiser.

***

Out front, the soldiers had given up chasing Inder and now surrounded the tank. Inder stood on the turret, flexing his skinny arms.

"I am the tank king! It's my tank, *ha ha!*"

Behind him, the hatch lid slowly opened and a soldier climbed out. Ob and Gern shouted a warning, but it was too late. The tank commander grabbed Inder and lowered him to the waiting soldiers.

Regin, whose job had been to guard the bikes, watched from the hedge. That was it. He was the last of the Crescent Street bike club, gang, whatever...the last superhero. He looked down at his green superhero gloves. He had even drawn his lightning bolt logo on his matching green shoes. But here he was, hiding in the bushes while his teammates, his best friends were going down in a blaze of glory. Some kind of superhero he was. The fat kid, the slow kid...he felt completely helpless.

As he looked down at his shoes, the sun sparkled on a tear as it rolled off the lightning bolt. Not today. He clenched his teeth and mounted his bike.

***

Maksey, Shaley, and Chalo crept around the side of the house at the end of the street and behind the hedge, when they heard Regin give a mighty yell. They looked over the hedge and saw Regin fly down the street and straight at the soldiers. Sunlight flashed off of the tin foil shield on the front of his bike and the men had to shield their eyes from the blinding glare. Regin was larger than the other kids and the soldiers dived out of his way, letting him blaze through their ranks.

"Like a bolt of lightning." Chalo shook his head as he watched incredulously. "Come on!" He hopped onto his bike and pedaled into the fray with Maksey and Shaley on his tail.

As the soldiers were diving for cover, Ob, Gern, and Inder had broken free. Now they ran as hard as they could. Regin skidded to a stop in front of Inder.

"Get on!" he yelled at Inder. The boy climbed on just as Chalo, Maksey, and Shaley pulled up.

Ob and Gern hitched a ride with Shaley and Chalo while Maksey kept flashing her shield at the soldiers. It was a matter of seconds until the solders recovered, but by then, the bikes had been retrieved and the Crescent Street club, gang, whatever…was gone.

They swept into Chalo's driveway and pulled all of the bikes into the garage. Once they were safely inside the clubhouse it was cheers and high fives all around. They all felt like real heroes, and Regin got special honors.

"So, what do we do now?" Regin asked.

Inder nodded. "Yeah the soldiers will be looking for us now that we've humiliated them." A small cheer went up.

"We're not their main objective. It's the girls they're really after, and let's not forget that they still have their mother." Chalo looked at Maksey and Shaley who were getting more worried by the minute.

"Wait, I know." Shaley jumped up. "Constable Tember."

"The cops again?" Chalo paled. "I don't know, Shaley…"

"No, you don't understand, he and our mom, they're kind of seeing each other."

The boys were shocked.
"Okay, take it easy, people, settle down," Chalo broke in. "This is actually a good thing. It means the cops are on our side."

"Finally!" Ob and Gern cheered.

"You're not getting the point!" Maksey spoke up, frustrated with them all. "They showed the film on the news, but they took out you guys."

"What is she talking about?"

"They showed the film?"

"Who took us out?"

"They showed the film! I'm a famous film maker!"

"Settle down, Inder," Chalo scolded.

"The film on the news didn't show you guy throwing the rocks, just the rocks hitting Mr. Townes," Maksey explained. "They were making like it was the Olred army who was attacking him."

"Oh shik! That's why the army is here, they're trying to start a war with Olred."

Maksey nodded. "Exactly! That why we have to get the film and give it to the Constable. He'll know what to do!"

***

The soldiers kept Spence firmly in the little chair by pressing down on his shoulders.

"I can see you. That light isn't bright enough, just like you."

"That's enough out of you, young man! Where are your sisters?"

"Go stick your head in a hole."

"Now, that isn't the way a nice boy talks, especially to a man who might throw his mother in the slammer!"

"You're throwing *your mother* in the slammer? Why, for having you?"

"No! I mean…all right, kid, you think you're funny?"

The soldiers all left the room, leaving Spence alone, then Debry locked the door from the outside. "There, laugh if off for a while, funny boy!"

"Hey!" Spence got up and pounded the door, then quietly laughed to himself. "Fine." He put on the act of being irritated. "I'm not saying another word! I'm on a silence strike!" He opened his closet door and, using a technique he'd perfected years before, quietly slid down the laundry chute and escaped through the basement window. It was a regular passage for him.

He stayed behind the hedge next to the house as two soldiers walked past. When he was in the clear, he leapt over the fence and started through the maze of backyards and gardens, following a route that only he knew.

He had been the only kid in the neighborhood for many years and had needed to learn ways to get to his friends' houses across town. Now he made his way along the secret path that would eventually take him to the farm. There wasn't a street or alley Spence didn't know; the woods around Mortimer's farm had been his stomping grounds for years.

He even knew how to cross Namarin Road without being spotted: he used the culvert that ran under the road at the tree tunnel. He had to scramble on all fours through the shallow water, but he passed unseen to the fields beyond. After that, he followed the hedgerow into the trees. Once he was in the woods he could make his plans. Woe be to anyone who thought they could out-fox him in there.

***

"Whoa!" Bemis exclaimed as the cruiser pulled onto Mim's street.

"A tank? This is going too far." Tember made a visible effort to keep his anger at bay.

"Easy, Pal, remember, there's more than one way to un-tree a grat." The sergeant gave him a sly smile.

Their cruiser slowly eased by the tank then pulled into the neighbor's driveway.

"Ready for this?" Bemis gave his partner a wink.

"Lead the way, Sarge."

They got out and went to the neighbor's door. Two soldiers eyed them suspiciously, but Bemis just tipped his hat to them and rang the bell.

The door opened. "Yes?"

"Mrs. Merfy, could Constable Tember and I come in for a moment? We have some police business to talk to you about."

The woman was clearly shaken by the Army's presence in the neighborhood. They sat on the couch opposite Mrs. Merfy's husband while she brought hot drinks.

"Mr. Merfy, what do—"

"Keern."

"What's that?"

"Call me Keern, Keern Merfy—that's me name."

"Right, Keern, we have had some, uh, reports of unusual…um, things going on."

"Yer telling me! Fer frip sake! Half the bleemin army is crawling up me ards!"

"Um, yes, well, there is that…" Bemis stammered, and looked at Tember who cleared his throat.

"Um…I was wondering if I could use your bathroom," Tember said.

Mrs. Merfy had just set down the tray of drinks. "Of course, it's—"

"No, that's fine." Tember got up and moved to the stairway. "I know where it is, these houses all have the same layout. Thanks." He disappeared up the stairs.

Mrs. Merfy looked at Bemis. "But there's a loo down here."

"Oh, never mind him. He's just got a thing for…um, heights? Anyway, as I was saying…" Sergeant Bemis stammered, trying to distract her as Tember went upstairs and searched for the door to the attic.

He found it in the hallway ceiling. Using a chair from one of the bedrooms, he pulled himself up into the roof space. Dust swirled in front of his face, making him choke, but he pulled out his flashlight and crawled in the direction of Mim's house. In the wall of the attic, a small door connected the two houses.

He squirmed through and into Mim's attic. The rafters in there had a wide, dusty board nailed across them and led to a hatch that was similar to Mrs. Merfy's. Just as he'd said, the layout of the houses was practically the same.

Tember checked to see if the hallway was clear before dropping down. He opened the door to the girls' room with no problem, and did the same with Spence's. When he tried Mim's room, however, it was locked. He listened for anyone coming. When he was sure that the coast was clear, he used a special police prying tool on the lock. The tool did the job it was built for and the lock came off with little effort.

"Mim?"

"Pal? How did you…?" He swept her up and kissed her. "Wow…" she sighed.

"Let's go." He checked the hallway, then boosted her into the attic.

He could hear boots climbing the stairs.

There was no chair this time, and Tember struggled to pull himself up into the space. Mim reached down and pulled with all her might, but he only managed to get up to his elbows. The soldiers' voices grew louder as they climbed the stairs.

"Pretty good coffee."

"Yeah, but mine needs sugar."

"Well, she's got sugar."

"Really?"

"Yeah, it's right next to the… Oh, for cryin out loud, it's like looking after a raw recruit. Come on."

The steps went back down the stairs. Tember gave another mighty heave with Mim pulling under his arms and finally got himself into the attic. She slipped the hatch lid into place and they both froze. The soldiers had returned.

"Much better… Hey, what's all this dust?" The voices were right underneath them.

"I dunno. Maybe that's how the girls escaped."
One of the soldiers poked at the hatch with his rifle. Mim slid out of the way and silently landed in Tember's arms.

What the heck, Tember thought, *if we're gonna get caught, it might as well be fun.* He planted a long kiss on her.

"They'd never get up there. We'll find 'em," the other soldier grunted.

"Yeah, they'll turn up. How long can a little girl stay away from home anyway? It'll get dark soon, then we'll have them." The soldiers walked off.

Mim came up for air. "We should go."

***

"…and then I found the Constable at his desk the next morning, covered in donut crumbs! I knew then what had happened. It was all a matter of good detective work."
The Merfy's were getting tired of Bemis' rambling.

"So, why exactly are you here, Sergeant?" Mr. Merfy interrupted. "And where is that Constable of yours? I better go make sure he's okay."

"No! I mean, no, he's fine. He's been, um, having difficulty lately with his…um…"

"Say no more, I know what that's like. When I wake up in the morning it takes me fifteen minutes to even get a decent stream going."

"Keern, please, I don't think the Sergeant was talking about that."

"Well, I'm goin' ta check on him anyway. Maybe he wants some of my pills." Before Bemis could do anything, Mr. Merfy was on his way up the stairs. Bemis leapt to his feet and followed, but Merfy stopped halfway up and shouted, "What the blazes?"

Bemis put his head in his hand; they'd been found out.
As Merfy backed down the stairs, Bemis heard Tember say, "Sorry, excuse me…coming through. Stand back now, he's dangerous!"

Bemis, now at the bottom of the stairs, looked up to see Tember carrying a rolled up rug with a pair of feet sticking out of it. "I caught the burglar, folks. He was just where we thought he would be. We didn't want to alarm you but we've been looking for this one for quite some time. Oh, he's a rascal this one. We'd better get him down to the station as quick as possible. Excuse me." He pushed towards the door. Mrs. Merfy had to sit to keep from feinting.

Bemis picked up where Tember left off. "You see, this whole visit was just an excuse to find the burglar in your attic. We knew he was there—"

"He's a woman!" Mr. Merfy pointed at a foot that hung out of the carpet.

"Oh no, he's just got, um…dainty feet. That's what they call him; The Dainty Foot Burglar."

"Why is he wrapped up in our rug?" Mr. Merfy eyed the bundle skeptically.

"Oh, we don't want you to see his face."

Bemis shrugged at Tember, and he took over again. "That's right, if you saw him you would be, uh…exposed, at risk from his criminal gang."

Mrs. Merfy sat up. "There's a criminal gang in Legly?"

"What? Oh, yes, ma'am, all around us."

Mrs. Merfy feinted again.

"But don't worry, Constable Tember and I are on the job."

"Bye now!" Tember trotted out to the cruiser with Mim who was trying hard to keep from laughing in the rolled up rug.

Bemis fired up the cruiser and they zoomed away, leaving Mr. Merfy standing in the door, scratching his head.

"Fer frip sake," he cussed, "crim'nals in the bleemin loft. Wadder you lookin' at, ya army knuckleheads!"

Chapter 10

Sitasti kept his lidless eyes on the military activity. Everything was going perfectly. The natives were about to declare war on each other. Once they wiped each other out, the planet would be his, every rock, tree, and ocean. As long as the natives didn't see him, he would still be within the confines of the law. When he finally made his claim public, he would be wealthy beyond his wildest dreams. The record would show that he was legally protecting a native from an off-world attacker. Was it his fault the stupid primitives blew each other out of existence? No, not his problem, just convenient that's all, and the court couldn't put him away for that. He would walk away the richest man in the sector.

His tongue flicked in and out as he thought of what he would do with his newfound wealth, but a sudden noise broke his daydream. There was someone there, someone close by. There, a native!

Sitasti had been so preoccupied he'd forgotten his chameleon camouflage. Now the native boy had seen him. Sitasti scrambled on all fours and caught up with the fleeing boy. He overtook the child and rose up in front of him, scaring him to a standstill. Then, when his target was frozen with fear, he coughed up a dark mass of toxic catarrh with deadly accuracy.

***

Spence had been making his way to a quiet area in the trees where he'd camped many times before, but as he approached the place, he knew someone was there. Quietly, he pulled aside a leafy branch to get a better look. His heart froze at the sight of some kind of giant alligator as it turned and looked straight at him.

Before Spence even made the decision, his legs sprang into action. Fear blew the craftiness right out of him as he crashed headlong through the undergrowth without thinking about all the paths he knew. Scratched and bruised, he heard the giant reptile right on his heels. Any minute he knew he would feel those claws in his back.

Suddenly he realized that he couldn't hear the creature chasing him anymore. He'd lost it! He looked back and sure enough, it wasn't there. Relieved, he slowed to catch his breath. That's when the creature appeared right in front of him.

Spence froze as the giant reptile reared back on its hind legs and opened its huge jaws, then everything went black.

The last thing Spence thought was that it wasn't so bad getting eaten by a reptile. It didn't even hurt.

***

Sitasti tied the native's hands with an IdentiStrip, then called his ship. The onboard computer would home in on the IdentiStrip's signal and use its tractor beam to hoist the native up. Sitasti had included instructions for the youngling to be stored in a locked compartment. As the child was hoisted up to the ship, Sitasti returned to his work at the shield that was protecting the old man.

He'd keep the young native unconscious until he could figure out how to erase the boy's memory. There were ways of doing such things, none of them pleasant, but then Sitasti had too much riding on this to have it ruined by some pesky native boy. At least, for now, he would be out of the way, safely stashed away as a prisoner of GMD Fives and Nines.

***

"Sir! The prisoners are gone!" the radio crackled.

"What?" Debry was driving back to the farm. "You idiots! It was a woman and a teenager, how did you let them escape?"

"Well, sir, we—"

"I don't actually want a description, you shikhead! It was a rhetorical question!" Debry threw the radio microphone to the floor in frustration, but the coiled cord sprung it back into his face. He batted at the radio, grabbed the microphone, and tore it off. "DRIVER! Take me to that farm!"

"I'm going as fast as I can, sir."

"Well go faster!"

"That's physically impossible, sir."

Debry fumed in the back seat as the car finally drove past Mortimer's house. The old man was working away, painting the shed. The sight of him made Debry all the more furious. As the car pulled up to the tent, he sat in the back seat for what seemed like an hour. The driver came around and opened the door.

"At last! What took you so long?"

"I was going—"

"I know, I know, as *fast* as you *can*. Bleemin' dape." He stomped into the tent and cracked his shin on the stump that was the main table. "Arrgh! WHO PUT THAT THERE?"

"Uh…"

"Don't. Say. It." He leveled his finger at the guard's nose, then sat down to nurse his shin. "Get me Central on the vox."

A soldier handed him a phone receiver.

"This is Debry. Get me Central Command. General Puxley? Debry here. They haven't cracked it, sir. The brains say that the technology is way beyond us."

The General's voice could be heard echoing from the vox. "I don't care what those crackpots tell you! If Olred can invent it, we can figure it out! I want you to escalate, see what it can take!"

"But it seems that the more we hit it, the bigger it gets."

"Maybe the bigger it gets, the weaker it gets. It has to have a limit. Everything has limits, Debry, including my patience. I said escalate, Debry, ESCALATE!"

"Yes sir." Debry handed the receiver back to the radioman. "He wants results? He wants escalation? I'll give him escalation. Private, get me Air Command."

The radioman handed Debry the receiver again. "This is Debry. I want a Decimator on target zero in five minutes." He handed the receiver back to the radioman. "This should wake up the neighbors."

The camp began bustling with activity. Soldiers took cover and vehicles were moved. Soon Debry stood in the tent doorway wearing sunglasses and a helmet.

"Any time now."

"Sir, you should take cover."

"And miss the moment that makes me the greatest military leader in history? Nonsense, soldier."

Suddenly, the entire army camp began to move of its own accord as the invisible shield started to grow and push outwards. Vehicles tumbled and rolled, tents were flattened under the invisible wall as soldiers stumbled out of the way. The shield grew over a hundred meters in seconds, throwing the army into chaos. Debry was tossed around inside the tent, narrowly avoiding being crushed by his car.

When the chaos finally stopped, he crawled out of the mangled tent, his helmet gone and his sunglasses bent and broken. Disoriented and swaying slightly, he stood up just as the jet thundered overhead.

"Oh shik."

The blast from the Decimator threw Debry twenty feet through the air. He landed in the mud outside the latrine tent and skidded to a stop. Everywhere was devastation. The bomb had knocked down a whole section of the forest that wasn't covered by the shield. Soldiers stumbled around trying to get their bearings while vehicles that had been set ablaze by the shockwave exploded around them.

Debry pulled himself up out of the muck and staggered over to the ruin of his command tent. From somewhere inside the pile of canvas and poles, a phone rang. A hand reached out through the pile of lumber that used to be Debry's bookcase.

"For you, sir," croaked the radioman.

Debry took the charred receiver. "Debry here."

"Well, is it still there?"

"Yes sir."

"Escalate! Dammit, Debry, I told you to escalate!"

"I did, sir, as big as it gets." Debry's head felt fuzzy and his vision was blurry.

"I don't care! I want bigger!" the General shouted.

***

Mortimer settled into his comfy old chair as Aga came out from the kitchen.

"The weather sure is doing strange things, Morty. All this thunder and flashes of lightning but no rain. I never seen the like."
Mortimer just smiled and kissed her hand as he took the meal. They said their prayer and settled down to watch the nightly news.

"The delegation from Olred has departed, saying that if the Fremian's aggressive attitude doesn't change then there may be no other option but war... Wait a minute, this just in.
"We interrupt tonight's broadcast to bring you the following exclusive from the Fremian government. The Fremian Counsel declares that the Olred Republic has been conducting espionage on Fremian soil and using its citizens in military experiments. These experiments look like the development of weapons of mass defense for use against Fremia and its allies.
"This action by Olred is a self-evident declaration of war. There is no other way to respond to this declaration than by answering with our own declaration. As of this evening, we, the Fremian people, are in a state of war with the Olred Republic.'
Mortimer reached out for his wife's hand.
Outside, Debry put down the receiver. "You have your orders, Captain, open fire."

***

Spence woke in a cramped space. He was on a rubbery floor in a hot and dark closet. His face felt squeaky clean and there was a strange taste like soap on his lips.

"Hey! Let me outta here!" He stood and pounded on the door. Suddenly, the door opened and a pair of huge, bright green eyes appeared out of the blinding light. "What the—"

"No, prisoner," chimed a pleasant, monotone voice.

Spence ducked under the floating eyes and out into the light. As he adjusted, he took in his surroundings. He was in something like a bright hotel room with no windows and slick surfaces everywhere. The floor was the same rubbery material. It was squishy to stand on but still gave him some traction.

"I'm not your prisoner! Who are you?"

The eyes followed him into the room. They were attached to a cluster of robotic arms suspended on a track in the ceiling. The arms reached for him, but Spence was quick. He had played similar games on the field at school and he ducked around the arms until they became crossed up.

"Stop moving," the voice intoned.

"Whatsa matter, too fast for ya? Can't catch me? Your one slow robot!" Spence dodged and weaved around the arms until they stopped reaching for him.

"Alternate strategy, negotiation."

"Oh, you want to talk now? Fine, tell me who you are and where I am."

"GMD Fives and Nines secondary lunar orbit. Thun."

"What the shik are you talking about?"

"Identity and location."

"Wait, your name is GMD?"

"Fives and Nines. Yes."

"Who named you, another robot?"

"Yes."

"Figures. Okay." Space narrowed his eyes at the thing and folded his arms. " So, GMD, what is fives and nines? Where are we, and why does my face feel weird?"

The robot's arms tucked in as it spoke. "Answer one: Fives and Nines is a part of my name. Apparently, when I was a prototype, my creator named me during a conversation in a card game. For some reason the voice imprint captured part of an arbitrary conversation.

"Answer two: Secondary lunar orbit. Thun.

"Answer three: The paralytic digestive adhesion that was used on you is the primary biological weapon of the gleekrin. Gleekrin gestate the compound in an organ specifically evolved for the task. The mixture is then coughed up at a high velocity at the intended victim with the intention of covering its breathing passages. Paralysis is instant and can last for several days unless the compound is removed. Yours was removed due to life-support concerns."

"Okay, wait." Spence held up a hand to pause the thing. "Something was stuck to my face? Is that what that reptile did?"

"Paralytic digestion adhesive is used to stun prey, keeping it fresh until consumed. Your metabolism reacted to the paralytic in such a way as to cause a high probability of cardiac arrest; life-support systems recommended removal in order to preserve the master's catch."

Spence didn't like being referred to as anyone's 'catch', but he shrugged. "So, I was going to have a heart attack if you didn't take that stuff off me? I guess I owe you one, thanks."

"Gratitude. Uncommon. Response unknown."

"Just say 'you're welcome'. Geez, doesn't anyone have manners anymore?"

"You are welcome."

Spence smiled at his minor success in altering the robot's programming. "You said we're in orbit around something called a *thoon*. What the heck does that mean?"

"You do not understand the data concerning your location. I will show you."

The floor went transparent.

"Holy shik!"

Spence was confronted with the vastness of space stretching out at his feet. Startled, he jumped back and pressed against the wall behind him. It took a minute to take in what he was seeing. Even in a state of shock, he recognized the smaller of the two moons rotating steadily beneath them.

"W-wow!" he stammered. "We're in orbit around Danos!"

"If that is your name for the smaller of your two moons, then you are correct. Escape without death is impossible," GMD intoned.

In the distance, the planet and the large primary moon floated like jewels in a sea of stars. Spence just stared, shaking. "O…okay, you can close the window now."

"You understand?"

"Yes, GMD, just close the bleemin window!" The floor turned back to its original, dark opaque color. "So, you must belong to that reptile thing I saw in the woods."

"Master Sitasti. Yes, he is the owner of this vessel."

"Okay, so he must have sent me up here."

"That is correct."

"Why? Is he gonna eat me?"

"Possibly. Though Master's usual diet consists of various invertebrates within the arthropod phylum that have a chitinous exoskeleton—"

"In other words, bugs. So I'm not for dinner, but what does he want with…hold on, I get it now. I caught him." Spence's eyes lit up as he remembered. "He's the one causing all the trouble. Maksey was right, there was a snake-man before this reptile guy showed up, and a shield and everything! But why? If either of them is bad news, why not just blast us all with a death ray or something?"

"Section Ten of Galactic Law states that in the case of planetary prospecting, the only instance where a non-native is permitted on the undeveloped planet is to protect the natives from deliberate harm by a non-native intelligence. In such a case, any detection of the protecting party by natives is deemed punishable by life imprisonment."

"You mean if your master was protecting us from something else he'd be in the clear? Oh, from the snake-man. But he can't be seen or he gets life anyway. That's why he sent me here. I saw him. But wait...so the snake-man was trying to kill the farmer? That doesn't make any sense. GMD, what record do you have of any intelligent snake-type creatures landing on this planet?"

"Access forbidden to any species of the known galactic sector other than Master Sitasti."

"Hmm..." Spence thought for a second. "GMD, are we in the known galactic sector now, where your master is from?"

"No."

"Are there any of my species in the galactic sector your master comes from?"

"No."

"Then I'm not a species from the known sector. Access is permitted."

The robot dangled from the rails on the ceiling and made a clicking noise for a second. "My logic circuits concur. Species similar to your planet's snake species are as listed. One: grulgariat assassin. Name: Ilgut. Captured and taken into off-planet custody by the Unified Galactic Police."

"Ha ha! Busted! He's already been caught! So if this Sitasti character isn't actually protecting us from the snake assassin..." Spence wracked his brain but couldn't put the pieces together. "GMD, what is Sitasti doing on my planet?"

"Master Sitasti owns the rights to all of Thun's resources. The existence of an intelligent native species prevents him from actively selling that claim. By defending one native inhabitant it legalizes his presence, which he is using to cause the two largest factions on your planet to go to war, thereby exterminating the species and giving him legal rights to the planet and all of its resources."

Spence's shoulders slumped—exterminating the species? "I'm guessing that would make him rich?"

"Extremely."

Shik. Spence was the only one who knew what was really going on. He had to think quickly. He looked up at the robot, which at the moment was the only potential ally he had. "Do you think he's gonna keep you around once he gets rich?"

GMD's lights blinked at him. "Logically he will upgrade…"

"Leaving you to rot in the junk pile."

"I am not permitted to commit acts of self-preservation, if that is what you are implying."

"How about the ship?"

"In the absence of a qualified biological unit I am permitted to conduct maneuvers to preserve the operational integrity of this vessel."

"How about when an unqualified biological unit is aboard?"

"Then my directive is to assist the biological unit in the operation of this vessel."

Spence cracked a smile. "Then I hereby state that the only way to preserve the operational integrity of this ship is to land on the surface of the planet Thoon, country of Fremia, county of Vangs, town of Legly, on the farm of Mortimer Townes."

"But that operation will reveal the identity of Master Sitasti to the natives."

"And if they see him, then he loses possession of this ship, in which case the first person…sorry, biological unit, who claims it is the new owner, right?"

"In the absence of seizure by any other official means, yes."

"Then I, Spence, claim this ship to be mine. I already saw him, his cover is blown, so he loses the ship!"

GMD ticked and twitched for a moment. "My logic circuits…somehow…make sense of that reasoning. Extraordinary, Master Spence. Engaging primary drive to aforementioned destination."

Chapter 11

"Shaley, slow down!" Maksey pedaled as hard as she could but she just couldn't keep up. Regin stayed with her, partly because he was a true hero, the gang had given him special honors to prove it, but mostly because he was winded as well.

Breathing hard, they pulled up next to the gang outside the news station.

"Same plan. You guys distract, we'll go in and find the film." Chalo was all business.

"I got this one, boys." Shaley sauntered up to the front doors.
At the reception desk, a secretary looked at her over her glasses, but Shaley wasn't intimidated, she had the power of the tattle-rant.

"I'm here to tell the news about those soldiers who broke into my house, stole my mom, stole my brother and my sister, and ate all our food! They were even peeing on the bushes, and when I left they were gonna fry our grat on the outdoor grill. I have all the names of all the soldiers who are doing all of this…" she rambled on.

The whole gang snuck in the front doors, staying low as they crept behind Shaley and into the hallway behind the reception desk. They worked their way through the newsroom then fanned out to find the film.

Chalo paused before they split up. "Two minutes, meet back at the front. Failure is not an option."

They nodded and split. Maksey entered the maze of news desks and cubicles. One by one she looked on every desk and even checked in the meeting rooms, but she couldn't find the film. Just as she came out of one of the rooms, a news lady stopped her.

"Well hello, what's your name?"

"I'm not supposed to talk to strangers." Maksey walked off and quickly turned and went through a door just to get away. As she entered the little room she froze. A man stood with his back to her, inches away. He was cutting film and the floor was littered with it.

"Shut the door," he said without turning around. "I'm busy in here."

Maksey stepped in and closed the door. She stood still as a statue while the man hummed to himself and worked away. Every time he turned, she turned with him, staying behind his back. The room was only as big as a small closet, and as he snipped, pieces of film dropped on her head.

Finally, he turned all the way around and Maksey shuffled behind him. He opened the door, turned the light off, and left. Maksey waited until the door closed then turned the light back on. There was film all over the floor she started looking for the lost footage. She decided to look at the longer strips first.

Suddenly the door opened.

"Maksey!" It was Ob.

"Get in!" She pulled him inside and closed the door. Together they started to go through as much of the film as they could.

The door opened again.

"Maksey? Ob!" It was Gern.

They dragged him inside. Soon they were shoulder to shoulder, looking at filmstrips.

"Hey, I think this is some of it!" Ob held up a piece of film.

"Where did you find it?"

"Here, in this pile."

Maksey picked up the pile and stuffed it into her pockets as the door opened one more time.

"Hey, what are you kids doing in here?"

Maksey screamed and ran, followed by Ob and Gern. They sprinted through the halls and out the front door where Maksey ran smack into Chalo. She continued to jump up and down screaming.

"Maksey! Hey! Calm down!" Chalo had her by the shoulders. "Did you get it?" She nodded. "Then let's ride."

They piled onto their bikes and pedaled hard back to the clubhouse. Maksey had no problem keeping up this time. Once inside, they piled up the filmstrips and all gathered around, searching through them one by one.

Slowly the pieces of the cut scene took shape. Chalo sent Ob to get a roll of clear tape to stick them all together with. By the time they were done, the sun had gone down and scraps of tape and film covered the floor. Finally, they could play the cut scenes on the projector.

Even though it lasted only a couple of seconds, the footage clearly showed the boys in the frame, throwing rocks at Mortimer. Chalo was about to gather them together at the planning table when they heard a car pull up outside the house.

"Lights off, everybody hide!"

The side door opened and was blocked out by a tall figure in a large hat.

"Come out, kids," the person boomed. "You'll have no trouble from me, I'm here to help."

Maksey came out of hiding. "Constable?"

The light came on. It wasn't the constable. He reached out and picked Maksey up who screamed at the top of her lungs.

"Easy there, little one, I'm not going to hurt you. Calm down. I have a daughter just about your age. Her name is Paxy."

Maksey stopped screaming and squirming.

"My name is Halkus Moore, I'm a Special Inquisitor, which means I make sure the army and the police are doing their jobs and treating people fairly. Are you okay?"

Maksey nodded.

"Alright, I'm going to put you down but please don't run away. If you do, I won't be able to help you." He set Maksey down on the floor. "The rest of you can come out too. I meant what I said, I'm a friend and no one here is in any trouble."

Chalo came out first but stood back. "How do we know you're telling the truth?"

"Well, let's see. You're probably trying to find out where these two girls' mother is, right? And I would hazard a guess that you'd like to say a thing or two to the shik-brain who took over their house, wouldn't you? Well, I would too. As a matter of fact, I know him pretty well, and I can tell you, he doesn't like me very much. I'm the one who's going to put him away once I gather enough evidence.

"That's what I'm doing here. I'd like to know how you kids fit into the story. I need your part of it to fit the puzzle together and maybe get the good guys out of trouble and put the bad guys where they belong, in jail. I suspect, looking at your gear, that you are good guys. Am I right?"

The other boys had come out and stood behind Chalo. "We're the Crescent Street bike…gang," Chalo said.

"Club," Ob offered.

"Superheroes," Gern corrected.

Regin shrugged. "Whatever sounds better."

Halkus looked at them with respect in his eyes. He knew heroes when he saw them.

"How about the Crescent Street Riders? I can file it in the system and make it official. You would be recognized by the government as a Legly neighborhood watch group."

"Huddle," Chalo called.

It took only three seconds for the boys to agree. Finally, they had a complete name. They all piled onto the couch and told Halkus their story from beginning to end, then showed him the footage. Halkus listened patiently, only asking questions to clear things up.

When they were finished, he asked, "So what's your next move?"

"We were going to find the Constable and show him the missing footage. We figured if anybody could get it into the right hands, he could."

"Well, you're absolutely right. The Constable is a good man and he would have delivered the film to me. But, since you've taken it this far, I think you should finish it. I suggest we go down to the television station and, with a little persuasion, maybe you can get them to broadcast the correct footage. What do you think?"

"Do you want us to get into your car with you?" Maksey looked worried.

"No, definitely not. You should never get into cars with strangers and we only just met. You ride your bikes down and I'll meet you there. How does that sound?"

"Then will you help me find my mom?"

"Yes, of course." He looked up from Maksey to address the Crescent Street Riders, his voice resonating with sincerity. "Then we will find Maksey and Shaley's mother."

For the second time that day, the Crescent Street Riders saddled up on a mission. The Inquisitor made sure they passed through the military blockade with no hassles. As they whizzed past the soldiers and snaked their way through sandbagged emplacements, Maksey felt like she was a secret agent.

They met up with Inquisitor Moore at the TV station and all of them walked in the door with the imposing figure of Halkus standing behind them. The secretary looked up from her magazine, peered over the rim of her glasses, and froze.

"You!"

Shaley smiled at her across the desk. "Hello again."

"Special Inquisitor Moore." He flashed his badge. "The news studio. Which way?"

"Oh, I'm...uh, not sure I can let you..." the secretary stammered.

The Inquisitor's gaze narrowed, boring into the startled woman.

Her snippy façade crumbled. "Yes, sir, right this way."
She led them through a maze of corridors and through a large metal door.

"But their broadcasting right now, sir! You can't…"

Halkus burst into the studio like a storm. The kids were on his heels, delivering polite waves to the stunned crew. The Inquisitor didn't stop; he strode onto the set, picked Maksey up and sat her on the edge of the desk right in front of the news anchor. He only turned briefly to say, "Excuse me."
The anchorwoman got up and scurried away.

"Kindly continue broadcasting please," Halkus instructed the crew, then faced the camera. "Good day. My name is Halkus Moore. I am a Special Inquisitor with the Fremian Counsel. Over the last several days we have been shown misinformation that has led us to disagreements, and finally to declare war with our Olred neighbors.
"I have been tracking the chain of events that have led up to this situation and there have been some links missing in the story. A short time ago I discovered a key link, one that I believe will cause us to reconsider our position and possibly affect our choices about the future."

The children piled onto the desk around him. The studio was dead quiet and all cameras focused on Halkus.

"This information came to light solely because of the efforts of these brave children who, in my eyes, are not children at all, but true heroes of not only Fremia, but our entire world. I believe I will leave the telling of this tale to them. Have patience, they're excited."

Maksey started, then Chalo took over. With each of them adding bits and pieces, they told, in short, the story of how they'd made the footage. Then Halkus finished off for them.

"So, to recap, the boys tested the shield and made a film of it. Somebody saw to it that the footage clipped them out of the picture to make it seem like the whole operation was an Olred intelligence mission, which it wasn't. What is still unclear, and I'm certain is a mystery to both Fremia and Olred, is what the shield is and why it is protecting this one, humble farmer. I leave you now with the footage. Look for the boys in the foreground. Thank you."

Halkus walked off the set and handed the footage to the producer, who took it into the film booth. Halkus waited in the studio with the children.

"Are we done now?" Maksey looked up at him.

"Not quite, little one, we still have a rat to trap." He smiled as a few minutes later, two large agents in the same long black coats and big hats that Halkus wore, dragged the producer back into the anchor room.

"We caught him trying to switch the film. Here's the cut version, sir. The real one is playing right now."

They looked at the monitor as the footage showed the boys throwing rocks at Mortimer's back, over and over.

"He made me do it!" the producer wailed. "That army guy. He said he would take over the whole studio if I didn't do it!" The producer fell to his knees, groveling.

Halkus knelt down until he was nose to nose with the man. "Name."

"Deadry or Deggy or something. Don't kill me, please!"

One of the agents stifled a laugh. Halkus looked at Maksey and Chalo, and tilted his head at the producer. Maksey stepped up to him while the cameras continued to roll.

"You're a bad man!" She stuck her tongue out at him.

Chalo stood behind her. "And the Crescent Street Riders don't like bad guys."

Halkus took Maksey's hand and they all strode out of the studio. "Play it on the hour, every hour," he barked as they left.

Chapter 12

"Take the back roads," Tember said.

The cruiser swerved around the sandbagged gun emplacements in the middle of the street. Everywhere there were soldiers and army units, missiles and heavy armor.

"They're tearing up our town." Bemis shook his head and worked the wheel of the big cruiser. In the back, Mim held onto Tember, worried sick about her children.

"They're probably scared to death with everything that happened at the house," Tember said, "but don't you worry, we'll find them."

"I hope so. I think Maksey will go to the woods to hide, and wherever Maksey goes, Shaley is right behind," Mim nodded.

"And what about Spence?"

Mim laughed a little hysterically in her concern. "Spence knows this town better than anybody. He practically owns those woods. I bet he's in there right now with Maksey and Shaley. Don't you think? Oh, I hope so, Pal. I hate the thought of my little angels in the woods all alone."

"Heck, they probably have a nice fire going with hot drinks by now, Mim," he reassured her. "I think your little angels are very capable. After all, look at their mother." Tember sat up quickly. "There! Take this road." He pointed over Bemis shoulder.

"But it's a tractor path!"

"Take it!" He reached over, grabbed the wheel, and spun it to the right. The cruiser screeched into the turn.

"All right, don't get grabby!" Bemis pushed Tember's hand away as he corrected his steering. The cruiser leveled out again. "Now where?"

"Slow down, we don't want to kick up dust. That's it, now just creep us into those trees. This will put us on the east edge of the woods, behind the shield and opposite the army."

The cruiser rolled quietly to a stop and they climbed out. Mim was still in her jammies, robe, and slippers. In the trunk, Tember rummaged through a pile of firearms, tossing a shotgun and radio to Bemis.

"Here, Mim, put this on." Tember gave her his police jacket.

"We should start back at Maksey's 'slimy tree'. You know, the one she saw the snake-man in? I think that's the most likely place she would go," Mim suggested.

"Sarge," Tember called to Bemis, "you head along the north edge of the woods and see how close you can get to the western perimeter."

Bemis gave a nod and trotted off through the trees. Tember and Mim set off along a different track.

"Walking through the woods in my slippers. You really know how to sweep a girl off her feet," Mim joked.

"Once we find our kids and get this mess figured out, I'll do the job properly." Tember concentrated on pushing through the undergrowth, not noticing how Mim stumbled a little after hearing him say 'our' kids.

"There, I think that's it up ahead." Mim realized, and pushed forward into the clearing by the slimy tree.

"This is where she said she saw the snake-man," Tember said, frustrated.

"They're not here," Mim deflated.
Tember clenched his teeth. "It's alright, we'll keep looking. Maybe

Sarge has found them." He keyed the radio. "Sarge, come in, over." He scowled when he got no reply. "Sarge, this is Tember, are you there? Over." He shook his head. "Nothing. These radios have a good range. There shouldn't be a problem raising him. Something is wrong."

***

Bemis broke out in a sweat only six meters from where he left Tember and Mim behind, so he slowed his jog to a fast walk. The undergrowth slapped him in the face and tore at his jacket as he pushed through.

"I'm out of shape for this kind of thing! Time to start thinking about retiring, Sarge," he muttered to himself, but the thought of retiring as a sergeant just grated on him.

He should be a Lieutenant, like the man he'd replaced. He had been running the Legly station for over fifteen years without a promotion or a raise. Now here he was, out in the woods on the most exciting case in the history of the county, and all he could think of was quitting.

"Shikhead!" he chastised himself. "You used to be better than this. Well, there's gonna be a few changes around here. Time for Sarge to earn his stripes."

He swatted at the dense foliage with his shotgun, battering his way through the leaves. Suddenly, he burst out into the open and stumbled over something…something that hissed.

He rolled quickly onto his back, just in time to see a black glob of goo smack him hard in the face. He felt instantly sick and woozy, then everything went black.

***

The end was soon, Sitasti could taste it. War had been declared and the armies were ready to strike each other down. He just had to keep the shield up a little longer and it would all be over. The only thing he hadn't anticipated was that the larger the shield got, the more often it needed to charge, but that was easily remedied. He unfolded the receiver array and held it up to get a signal. Nothing.

"Come on, GMD fives and nines, where are you?" He moved around, trying to get a connection. Nothing happened. Something was wrong, where was the ship? It was scheduled to be in orbit above him right now.

He checked the shield generator. It would only hold for another hour at this rate. He held up the control unit, and again, searched for a signal. If he could just make a connection, the shield generator would recharge in a matter of minutes.

A noise distracted him and he looked up just as a short, fat native came plowing through the brush and crashed over the generator, sending it and Sitasti sprawling. The huge reptile jumped to his feet and spat, knocking the native out so he looked like a sleeping slug. Sitasti smiled a wide, toothy grin. These natives were so weak. They had no natural defenses. It was a shame he couldn't confront them all, it would be so easy to take them out.

He picked up the shield generator and set it back upright. It was a sturdy, military-grade piece of hardware that could take a beating. Sitasti dusted it off, picked up the control unit, and resumed searching the sky for a signal. Suddenly, a short beeping came from the shield generator. It was a low-charge warning. The army was shelling the shield again and it drained the power quickly. He had to find that signal, but as he held the controller up again, a searing pain shot through his arm and the controller went flying into the woods.

Tember pushed Mim behind him. "Freeze you…whatever you are!"

Sitasti stretched to his full height and gave a roar. The primitive had shot him! A fan of scaly skin stood out from his neck, flashing an array of bright colors and making him seem twice his normal size. It would be another hour before he could spit again so he'd have to take down this one the old fashioned way. He spread his arms wide, revealing long claws, then dropped and charged towards Tember.

Tember shot again but the giant reptile was on all fours and the bullet just bounced off his tough hide.

The native waited until the last second, then dived out of the way as Sitasti pounced. Sitasti skidded and slung out a claw, missing by a millimeter. The man was quick, he thought, but no match for him. Sitasti recovered and lifted a large rock over his head. He would crush the primitive worm!

Tember scrambled to his feet only to look up and see the rock rising above him, but the creature just stood there. Colors and patterns flashed all over his body, then three bright red holes in his chest started to ooze blood.

Tember turned. Mim knelt over the sergeant's unconscious body, his shotgun smoking in her hands.

THE SHIELDING OF MORTIMER TOWNES

***

The big black Inquisitor cruiser roared up to the command tent with a trail of news crews right behind. The doors flew open as Halkus, the Crescent Street Riders, and another Inquisitor spilled out. The army was reloading for another barrage at the shield.

Halkus shouted into the command tent, "Major Pom Debry, by order of the Special Inquisition of the Fremian Counsel, I order you to cease fire at once! Stand down, men, no one fires another shot!" His voice boomed out across the encampment.

Debry stormed out of his hastily reconstructed tent. "What is this? You have no authority!"

"I was given the authority when I recovered evidence that proves you bribed the television producer to edit that clip."

"That proves nothing! We are at a state of war and this farm is an enemy research facility. Men, prepare to fire!"

Halkus grabbed Debry and was about to slap handcuffs on him when a screaming roar split the sky. Everyone looked up as an oblong, silver ship streaked towards them. Halkus dropped his fistful of Debry's shirt, pushed the kids behind the cruiser, and shielded them as best he could, while Debry stood, dumbfounded.

The ship barely cleared Mortimer's house and skidded heavily into the field, throwing dirt and rocks everywhere. It finally came to rest, the sharp nose just a meter away from the stump, the metal hull sizzling.

"It went through the shield!" A soldier cried out, pointing.

A door hissed open in the side of the vessel and Spence peered out. "Hey! You guys alright?" He jumped down out of the ship as his sisters darted from cover to reach him, hugging him tight. Chalo and the boys trickled out after them to marvel at the ship.

Tember's cruiser came barreling across the field with Sitasti hanging limply out of the trunk, and skidded to a stop next to the ship. Mim jumped out and embraced her children as they talked over each other to tell her everything that had happened.

Bemis lay unconscious in the front seat of the cruiser. Mim had tried to remove as much of the goo as possible but he was still out cold.

Tember stepped out and made his way towards Halkus' cruiser

just in time to see Debry trying to climb into the spaceship.

"Where do you think you're going?" He snatched Debry by the collar and handcuffed him. "I think this belongs to you," he told Halkus' as he shoved Debry against the Inquisitor's car.

"Watch him a minute will you? " Halkus asked Tember then turned his attention back to the radio. "Yes, Chief, a spaceship, that's right."

"You get that thing under wraps, Halkus, you understand?" the Chief said.

"I'm afraid it's a bit late for that, Chief, the news has broadcast the whole thing. Besides, the ship doesn't belong to us."

"What? Whose is it? What are they doing here and what do they want? And what do we do with the alien? Did you get the shield? Hold on a minute."

"Chief, I think you should—"

"Wait a minute, Halkus. We've got a development here. I'm patching you through."

"Hello, Inquisitor Halkus? I am Chugtang of the Unified Galactic Police. You seem to have solved our case for us, my congratulations."

For the first time in his career, Halkus didn't know what to say. "Uh...thanks?"

"If you could just remove the suspect from the vehicle, we would be happy to take him off of your hands."

Halkus looked at Tember who nodded and went to pull Sitasti out of the cruiser. "My apologies...um, Chugtang. It appears that he was killed during a scuffle with local law enforcement..."

"No, he's fine, I assure you."

"But he's got three bullet holes in his chest."

"Yes, but he's a gleekrin. The only vital organ they have is what you would probably relate to a brain, and that is located around the area of the...butt. Is that right? Butt. Yes, I think so."

"Um...I understand. We have a few of those down here as well." He glowered at Debry.

"We're hauling him up now," Chugtang said, as Sitasti rose into the air to gasps from the crowd.
Tember looked at Maksey with wonder as the family gathered near him. "Just like the snake-man, right?"
Maksey nodded.

Mim kissed her daughter. "I'll never doubt you again."

"Inquisitor Halkus," Chugtang broke through the radio again, "I'm afraid we'll have to confiscate the ship as well. It's databanks hold the evidence we need to wrap this thing up."

"I thought as much. Haul away," Halkus replied.

The ship rose slowly off the ground and into the sky. Spence looked crushed. Mim pulled him into the family hug.

"Aw honey, you did a great job," Mim said, "but look at that landing. Maybe we'll get you some flying lessons for your eighteenth birthday, whaddaya say?"

**

That evening, as the army packed up and moved out of Legly, Mortimer settled into his chair. Aga came in with the evening meal and placed it on the tray.

"Did you ever find out what all those people were doing over in the field, Morty?"

The news anchor came on the screen. "WLEG News at six, tonight; the biggest night of news ever. Officials declare a cease fire and cancel the state of war with Olred. Alien spaceship lands in Legly, and a group of kids called the Crescent Street Riders save the world."

Mortimer reached out and took his wife's hand. "Oh, they're fine, let them be."

The End

Just because you want to know…

Thun (known as 'Maina' to the natives) was officially added to the galactic register in its own brand new sector.

Fremia and Olred put aside their differences, and together dealt with galactic representatives who helped guide them along the path of peace.

Pal Tember married Mim and was recruited to become a Special Inquisitor.

Bemis finally got promoted to Lieutenant and became the Chief of Police in Legly.

No one knows what happened to Halkus Moore, but it's rumored that he may have found a position with the Unified Galactic Police.

Ilgut, Sitasti, and Drom live where it's dry and cold. They have life-long employment turning icebergs into ice cubes.

Spence took those flying lessons and became a pilot for the newly formed air force of the Maina Planetary Coalition.

Maksey has plans to become a police officer, just like her step-dad while Shaley wants to go into investigative journalism.

And the Crescent Street Riders? Well, they ride.

ABOUT THE AUTHOR

Musician, kayak guide, renaissance swashbuckler…Montgomery Thompson likes to do fun stuff. Born in Maryland and raised in Colorado, Monte claims Sandpoint, Idaho as his hometown; which is kind of confusing but hey! Ya gotta be from somewhere, right? Even more perplexing is that most of the time he can be found in the hills of Northern Ireland playing a tune, writing a word and buckling a …swash? Hmm, that is odd now isn't it?

His other works for kids include *The Christmas Wish Tree*.
For the grown-ups and fans of sci-fi action adventure be sure to read Montgomery's premiere works; *The God String, The Second Split* and *Augmentia*

All of these are, of course, available on Amazon.com and Amazon.co.uk

Printed by Amazon Italia Logistica S.r.l.
Torrazza Piemonte (TO), Italy